The Marquess of Temptation

Claudia Stone

DEDICATION

For Henry and his owner Claire, with love and best wishes for your next adventure.

CONTENTS

ABOUT THE AUTHOR

Claudia Stone has been obsessed by historical romance, ever since Forever Amber was banned in her secondary school. She loves every time-period, but her particular favorite is Regency.

Claudia is married to Conal, a dairy farmer and they have three boys…two of whom are still young enough to be "mortified" by her writing adventures, and one who is old enough to think his Mum is kind of cool (kind of).

1 CHAPTER ONE

"Never marry for love, Hestia. Love only works in fairy tales."

This was the sage advice that Hestia Stockbow's mother, Georgina, imparted to her almost daily, for the whole of her childhood.

"Love won't heat your home," Georgina would grumble mid-winter, when a damp chill permeated their small, stone cottage on the Cornish coast. "Or put food in your children's bellies. Do you understand me?"

Hestia would nod solemnly, taking in every word, whilst her mother worked furiously at the bellows, trying to get a flame to catch hold in the kitchen stove. Georgina Stockbow was a beautiful woman, her exquisite face topped by an abundance of golden curls, which Hestia adored brushing with the mother-of-pearl comb that Georgina kept on her dressing table. The comb was the final vestige of Georgina's previous life, and Hestia knew to handle it with the utmost care and respect.

Her mother had grown up as the only daughter of a Viscount and by all accounts had been adored by her parents. On cold evenings, when her father was away, Hestia's mother would regale her with tales of all the dresses and toys that she had owned when she was a girl. She made her previous life sound like a fairy tale; filled with large houses, glamorous people, elegant carriages and balls that went on until the wee hours of the morning. Unlike the story books that Hestia devoured, however, Georgina's fairy tale had ended when she fell in love.

"Now my life is just hard work, an aching back and a husband that's gone more than he's home," she would grumble, shooing Hestia away to bed. Poor Hestia, who was rather serious for such a cheerful looking child, took her mother's words to heart, and where other children feared the dark or goblins and ghouls, Hestia feared meeting Prince Charming, falling in love and being consigned to a life of drudgery.

Being a rather astute child, Hestia noted that while her mother loudly

1

and frequently protested that love was the most abominable thing known to man, she promptly forgot this the moment her father walked through the door. David Stockbow was a most handsome man; over six foot tall, with a shock of black hair, he always cut a dashing figure in his impeccable breeches and boots. Hestia would watch, with a rather detached amusement, as her mother would momentarily feign annoyance with him, for having left them for so long, before quickly falling under his spell, as he wooed her with the spoils of his travels. Silks, mink, and sometimes jewels would be placed on the kitchen table, like an offering for an olden day Empress, for her mother to inspect. Georgina would squeal with delight, fling her arms around her husband's neck and order Hestia outside to play for a few hours. Depending on the length of her father's stay, Hestia would end up spending rather a lot of time in the great outdoors, which she did not mind - but she did find it bothersome when he chose to return in winter.

Inevitably, when her father returned to sea, Hestia would be summoned back inside the confines of Rose Cottage to help her mother decide which of her father's gifts should be brought to the pawn shop in Truro first. Once everything that could be pawned was gone, Georgina would dress Hestia in her Sunday best and frog-march her through the countryside to pay Lady Bedford a visit.

"He's away again?" the old woman would say, with a sigh that wracked her whole body, when Hestia and her mother were ushered into the drawing room.

"You know I hate to ask..." Georgina would whisper.

"I do."

And so did Hestia. She knew from her mother's slumped shoulders and the deepness of the marionette lines, which dragged her smile into a frown, that asking Lady Bedford for help was almost as soul destroying an act as falling in love.

"I'll fetch my purse," Lady Bedford would sigh, before pointedly adding, "Your poor mother was right about him."

"I know," Georgina would whisper.

That Lady Bedford knew Georgina from her past life was a source of endless fascination for Hestia. Sometimes, when her mother was struck down with her mysterious, unknown ailment, Hestia was shipped off to Bedford Hall, to be looked after by her Grandmother's old friend.

"Tell me about my Grandmama," she would beg and Lady Bedford would duly oblige. The Viscount and Viscountess Havisham had adored their only daughter, nearly more than their only son. Which was unthinkable really, for girls were little more than a pretty accessory, designed to complement the male off-spring.

"They were heartbroken when your mother ran off with that

scoundrel," Lady Bedford never referred to Hestia's father by name, preferring to Christen him with new monikers like; that scoundrel, that reprobate, that pirate. "Your Grandfather insisted that she be cut off, though when I found out that you were living just outside Truro, your Grandmother often wrote to me, asking for news of you both."

"What did you tell her about me?" Hestia would ask, with wide eyes.

"That you were perfectly perfect," Lady Bedford would smile, "Even if you were born out of scandal…"

Lady Bedford detested scandal. Her own sister, Mrs Actrol, had brought great shame on her family by becoming a Bluestocking author. Hestia, in turn, adored Mrs Actrol, who when she visited, said things which made Lady Bedford cluck her tongue in disapproval. As the years went on and Hestia's mother spent more time in bed, afflicted by a mysterious illness that left her pale and wan, Hestia spent more and more time at Bedford Hall, reading aloud to Lady Bedford or walking one of her many King Charles Cavaliers.

"Lord Bedford detests dogs, he can't bear to be in the same room as them."

If Hestia thought it was rather strange that Lord Bedford's wife had thusly surrounded herself with no less than eight of the creatures, she kept it to herself. She had become much wiser about marriage as she grew; her own parents' tempestuous relationship had near ended since war was declared with Napoleon and her father had taken to sea. Not to fight for a noble cause, her mother would point out with annoyance, rather to plunder the ports of war stricken countries. Before he had left for, what was to be the last time in their marriage, Hestia had overheard her mother reading aloud from the paper.

"Do you see this David? My cousin Amelia has married a Marquess - Lord Delaney. What a sensible girl she always was and now she has married a man with means."

"You were never sensible, my love," Hestia's father had crooned in return, though rather than give a giddy laugh to his flirting, like she usually did, Hestia's mother had emitted a small sob. "No, I don't suppose I was."

By the time that Hestia turned sixteen, her mother had wasted away to skin and bone, and spent most of her days in bed. Hestia kept up her visits to Lady Bedford, both for the comfort that the warmth of Bedford Hall brought, and the few coins that the Lady of the house would slip into her palm as she was leaving. The few coins bought food and firewood, but what her mother needed more than either fuel or food, was a physician. One night, when her mother's breathing became shallow and erratic, Hestia penned a missive to the current Viscount Havisham of Kent, begging for funds to help his ailing sibling.

He arrived a fortnight later, a tall man with a shock of blond hair like his sister's. His face was awash with disapproval as he surveyed the small, stone cottage where his sister had raised his niece.

"I shan't pay a penny for her treatment," he said by way of greeting when Hestia opened the door, "She brought poverty on herself by marrying that cur, and the scandal sent my parents to an early grave. I won't pay for anything, do you hear me?"

"You won't have to spend a penny my Lord, for we buried her only yesterday," Hestia duly intoned, before shutting the door on the only member of her mother's family that she had ever laid eyes on.

Somebody, Hestia wasn't sure who, managed to get in contact with her father. He returned a month after Georgina's death, to fetch Hestia from Bedford Hall, where Lady Bedford had insisted she stay. He was unrecognisable from the man she had known; his hair was no longer black but grey, and his handsome face was concealed by a bushy beard that resembled Bedlam straw.

"You look so like your mother," he whispered, as he caught sight of Hestia for the first time in three years.

"Thank you," Hestia replied softly, shy of this strange man before her. Her father, once they were home in Rose Cottage, walked from room to room wearing a vacant expression.

"She's gone," he whispered, to which Hestia nodded. "I loved her, did you know?"

"I knew," Hestia refrained from sighing; oh how she knew about her parent's love for each other. Instead of finding strength from her father's presence, Hestia found herself playing the care-giver, as David Stockbow, the legendary adventurer, fell into a deep depression.

"I loved her so much," he would whisper, as he paced the house wearing his now customary vacant expression, his frame half starved with grief.

Love. Hestia deplored that word. Love had done nothing for anyone, bar cause misery and upset. Her father was unable to work, save for pottering around the garden, and once the treasures he had brought home with him were pawned, Hestia found herself once again paying daily visits to Lady Bedford.

"Can he not go out to work?" Lady Bedford would sigh, as she handed Hestia a fistful of coins.

"He can't seem to do anything," Hestia confessed from the corner of the room, where she was in danger of being smothered by what was now a dozen, boisterous Cavaliers. "He spends all day in the garden, building his…"

She trailed off; for she had no idea what it was her father was building. He had piled dozens of stones atop each other in the garden, before planting a bevy of wild roses around them. If she didn't know any better she would say he was building a shrine to her mother, but she did know better than to voice such concerns to Lady Bedford. Lady Bedford did hate a scandal - and nothing was more scandalous than a man losing his mind.

It was around the time of Hestia's nineteenth birthday, that her father's past came back to haunt him. Hestia returned home from Bedford Hall one evening, to find him hidden inside the cottage with all the shutters closed on the windows and the poker for the fire clutched in his hand.

"Has anyone in the village been asking after me?" he asked from a dark corner, his voice a low rasp.

"Not more than usual," Hestia replied diplomatically, for nobody in the village *ever* enquired after her father, though she hadn't the heart to tell him.

"I saw a man yesterday, a blond man, poking around the garden," her father licked his lips nervously. "And then I got a letter."

He gestured toward the kitchen table, upon which there was a page, much creased as though it had been read and folded a dozen times. Hestia glanced at her father, who was eyeing the page nervously and supposed that it had been manhandled more than once.

"I know what you stole, Stockbow," Hestia picked up the page and read aloud, trying to keep the note of alarm from her voice, "And I will kill you for it. Goodness, father, who sent this?"

"I don't know," her father's eyes were wild, "It could be anyone, Hestia. You're not safe here. You'll have to go back to Bedford Hall."

"I can't leave you," Hestia protested, though her father ignored her, waving his hand to silence her.

"You're not leaving me," he said, his voice firm and controlled, the voice he had spoken with when she was a child. The threat to his life seemed to give him strength and he visibly grew before her eyes. "I shall set off for Bristol at once. I'll send you on money, once I have it, until then stay with Lady Bedford."

He would broker no argument and Hestia soon found herself, for the second time that day, traipsing the country lane to Bedford Hall, where an unquestioning Lady Bedford had the maid show her to one of the less impressive guest rooms for the night. It was past midnight when the sound of voices from the entrance hall woke Hestia from her slumber.

"Dead as a doornail," she heard a deep voice boom, "Put a bullet through his head. Well, even you said that he had gone slightly mad since his wife passed, my Lady."

"How awful," Hestia heard Lady Bedford exclaim in response, "What an awful scandal for poor Hestia to bear."

What was an awful scandal? she wondered, creeping quietly down the grand staircase to where Lord and Lady Bedford and the local magistrate stood huddled together.

"What's an awful scandal?" she voiced, bile rising in her throat as the pale faces of the Bedfords turned to her.

"Your father has only gone and blown out his brains with a blunderbuss," Lord Bedford, who was hard of hearing and low on tact, bellowed so loudly that his words echoed off the cavernous ceiling of the entrance hall. Hestia felt as though the very ground beneath her had become unstable and she gripped the nearby banister to keep herself from falling.

"He can't have," she protested, "He was going to Bristol - he told me he was leaving for Bristol."

No matter how many times Hestia repeated this fact, she was ignored. Over the next few days her life was a blur of people traipsing in and out of Bedford Hall, speaking in whispers to the Lord and Lady of the house. She overheard the words "coroners court" and "suicide", spoken once or twice, and finally Reverend Plucker arrived to have a quiet word with her.

"We cannot bury your father on Church grounds, Hestia, I am sorry," he said, wiping his brow with a white linen handkerchief. "I would like to help, for you know how fond I am of you, but it's gone beyond my hands."

The only thing that Hestia found surprising in the Reverend's statement was to hear that he was fond of her, for previously he had barely even deigned to glance at her. She supposed that it was his job to offer kind words to the bereaved, though he evidently thought his job was finished, for he soon left.

A week after his death, her father was buried under the cover of darkness in unconsecrated ground just outside of Truro, beside criminals and thieves. Hestia was not present for the burial, though she intended to visit at some stage to pay her last respects, but then the papers caught wind of the story...

"It's a terrible scandal," Lady Bedford proclaimed, setting down the newspaper and looking at Hestia gravely. "I don't know what we shall do. Your name has been dragged, irrevocably, through the muddied waters of your father's life and death. I don't know what you shall do - no one will ever marry you."

Hestia, who had never thought of marrying anyone, picked up the newspaper curiously. On the front page there was a large caricature of her father as she had remembered him as a child, tall, strong and handsome, beneath a headline which read: "Verdict of Suicide Declared in Case of Notorious Privateer."

Underneath the headline was an in-depth article, describing, in great detail, the earlier scandal of her parent's marriage, her birth and her father's illustrious career as a thief of the seven seas. She read with wonder of his escapades in the Mediterranean during the War, the Egyptian treasures he had allegedly stolen from a Navy ship and how he had nearly died on numerous occasions, in spectacular ways. Had her father really been a pirate? This was all news to her. It would make sense, however, what with his penchant for disappearing to sea for years before returning with a haul of treasures for her mother.

"You cannot stay Hestia," Lady Bedford continued, jolting her from her reverie. "We shall have to send you away, somewhere no one will recognise you. Oh, this is indeed a terrible scandal."

Lady Bedford sent Hestia out to the gardens, to walk six of the dogs whilst she stayed inside and thought of a plan. By the time Hestia returned, her skirts muddied to her knees, the next chapter of her life had been plotted out by the industrious Lady Bedford.

"Mrs Actrol reliably informed me on her last visit, that the new Lady Jarvis is seeking a companion for her sister-in-law, Miss Jane Deveraux." Lady Bedford stated from her seat at her mahogany writing bureau. "I shall write to this new Viscountess with a glowing character reference for you — and include a few subtle reminders of my good standing in the ton, of course."

"Of course," Hestia echoed, her arms wrapped around the body of a squirming Cavalier. "Will she not recognise my name from the papers though, my Lady?"

"Clever girl," Lady Bedford exclaimed, "We shall have to give you a different name, my dear. Tell me, do you have a middle name?"

"Belinda."

"Belinda it is - and we shall simply tinker with your surname a little…"

And so, a fortnight later, Belinda Bowstock, with Henry, one of Lady Bedford's Cavaliers in tow, came to be employed as a companion to Miss Jane Deveraux, younger sister of the Viscount Jarvis. Jane was a bookish girl of nine and twenty, with a kind heart and no actual need for a paid companion.

"I'm afraid my new sister-in-law was afraid that she would have to spend time with me, so she hired you instead," Jane informed Belinda cheerfully on the first day of her employment. "I'm sure we'll rub along nicely together, though. Don't you, Belinda?"

It took Hestia a few moments to reply, for the sound of her new moniker was still so unfamiliar. Unfortunately there were several servants there to witness her slow response and it was quickly decided amongst them that the new girl was a featherbrain. Which suited Hestia quite nicely, for her brain was still reeling from her father's sudden death and the revelations about his history. Late at night, in the small bedroom on the top floor of the house, Hestia would mull over her father's last words to her and the letter he had received that fateful day. There were so many unanswered questions. Who was the blonde man that her father had seen in the garden? What was it that he had taken that had upset the letter writer so? And who was the mysterious author of the threatening letter in the first place?

Hestia resolved that once the fuss of the scandal had blown over, that she would return to Cornwall and find out exactly what had happened. For she knew, in her heart, that her father had not killed himself.

"I just need to keep my head down, like Lady Bedford said," she thought grimly, "And try to keep out of trouble so I can clear my father's name."

Which would have worked a treat, if Jane hadn't decided to bring her to a historical lecture in Bloomsbury, where trouble, in the form of the Marquess of Falconbridge, decided that it quite liked the look of Hestia B. Stockbow.

2 CHAPTER TWO

Alexander Jack de Pfeffel Delaney, Sixth Marquess of Falconbridge, was a man who liked reason and order. It stemmed, he thought, from his years of having studied the scientific art of mathematics. He fervently believed that everything happened for a reason and there was both a rational explanation *and* solution for any situation - until today, that is.

"How on earth did you manage to entangle yourself like that?" he drawled, his eyebrows knitted together in surprise as he surveyed the woman before him. The blonde lady, if one could call her that, for no proper lady would be skulking in Montagu House alone, was attached to one of the museum's ancient Greek urns by a long piece of ribbon, which was in itself attached to the most hideous bonnet Alex had ever seen. The ribbon had inexplicably wrapped itself into a knot around the slender neck of the urn and the young woman, who Alex estimated to be not more than twenty, was trying to detangle it without knocking over the priceless, historical artifact.

"I don't know," the girl stammered, turning toward his voice. Her movements caused the urn to wobble precariously and Alex uttered a silent oath. It would not do for her clumsy actions to break the artifact into smithereens. As a patron of the museum, Alex was well aware of the item's historical significance, not to mention value. He was also aware that the noise would send dozens of people scurrying their way - and then he would have to explain what he was doing, alone, in the pottery room with a young woman. A beautiful, young woman, if the parts of her that he could see, were anything to go by.

"Don't move," he ordered, absently touching her shoulder to still her. The problem, he deduced, began with the mammoth proportions of her awful hat. The bonnet was so large that it concealed her view, its brim acting like side-blinkers on a horse, and the poor girl must have panicked and tangled herself even more in a blind-tizz.

"We shall have to take off your hat," he declared confidently.

"I've tried that," a mournful voice replied, "There are so many pins holding it in place that it's near impossible."

"Nothing is impossible," Alex gently chided as he assessed the pins which, upon closer inspection, he now saw were threaded through the hair at the nape of the young woman's neck. It looked like there were at least two dozen of them determinedly binding the bonnet to her head.

"Why on earth do you need so many pins?" he wondered aloud, whilst thinking that it would take a few minutes of him threading his fingers through the young woman's locks before she was free. A thought that left him feeling a little dry-mouthed - which was ridiculous for a man of his age; he had touched far more intimate places on a woman's body than her hair.

"I need them to hold it in place, lest it's blown away by a gust of wind," the woman, whose face he still had not seen, explained cheerfully. "It's one of the chief risks of wearing a bonnet."

The opinion that losing the bonnet in question to a windy day, would, in fact, be no great loss, was on the tip of Alex's tongue, though he chivalrously refrained from voicing it. He knew that not everyone had the financial resources to be as sartorially refined as he, nor the help of London's most expensive valet in choosing clothes from Saville Row. Though heaven knows poverty was no excuse for such a heinous head-piece; the gift of sight was still free after all.

"I'm afraid, if I am to release you, that I will have to touch your hair," Alex said, the strange feeling inside him making him sound gruff and irritated. "I hope you won't take a fit of the vapours when I do."

"Lud, no," the girl snorted, "The only thing that's making me feel faint is the thought of that vase toppling over and breaking into a million pieces. My mistress would never let me hear the end of it."

"Your mistress?" Alex asked, as his fingers began to work their way through her hair. He wasn't particularly interested in the girl's life or occupation but he wanted a distraction from the alarmingly pleasant feeling of her gold locks against his fingers. Who knew that hair could feel so silky to the touch?

"Miss Jane Deveraux," there was a note of pride in the girl's voice, "She's here giving a lecture on the morality of the ancient Romans."

"Is she indeed?" Alex had little interest in the Romans - the Egyptians on the other hand were his current passion. He and his partner Pierre Dubois had been working since the war had ended, on trying to decipher the hieroglyphics found on an ancient Egyptian steele which was currently located in the museum. The work was a perfect mix of his two great loves - history and mathematics —for to decipher the ancient language required logic and Alex had that in spades.

"Oh, yes," the young woman nodded her head fervently, causing the pin in Alex's hand to snag on her curls. She did not seem to notice, for she continued speaking in her sing-song voice that brought images of the seaside in summer to mind.

"She knows everything about everything. She's so very clever - and she wants everyone else to be clever too. She helps to fund a school for girls in Brixton, so they can learn to read and write, and she spends her summers in St Jarvis attending egalitarian saloons with authors and poets."

"St Jarvis?" the woman's ramblings had finally caught Alex's attention, "Your mistress must be the Viscount's sister, Lord Deveraux."

"Are you acquainted?"

"In a way," Alex shrugged, he was nearly at the end of his bonnet mission, though his hands had now slowed and he was working at a more relaxed pace. There was something quite right about the feel of his fingers in this girl's hair and their close proximity. From where he stood he could feel the warmth emanating from her body and though he had not seen the young woman's face, he was certain it was pretty. What a pity she was only a servant...

"Everyone in the ton knows each other in some way or another," he continued absently, as he wrested the final pin attaching her bonnet to her head from her hair and - finally - set her free. "Especially the men. We either schooled together in Eton and Oxford, or served together on the continent."

"You served during the war?"

Alex was unable to answer the question, for, now that she was released, the woman had turned to face him, and her wide, blue eyed stare had left him feeling winded. He had been right, when he had thought she would be pretty, but now seeing her fully, he saw that he had also been wrong - this woman was more than that, she was beautiful. Not in the classical sense, though her hair was blonde and her eyes were blue as was currently fashionable, she was beautiful in a fragile, almost sad way, that left Alex longing to cradle her in his arms.

Goodness, he started, where on earth had that thought sprung from?

"I did," he replied with a shrug, "For a time."

For three years, in fact, until the death of his younger brother forced him back to English soil and into a hasty, ill-thought-out marriage. One did what one had to, to secure the line; though there was not a day that Alex did not regret leaving the men he had fought with behind. His guilt was assuaged by the fact that he had still been working for the crown, helping to decipher codes in correspondence from suspected spies, but first and foremost, he was a man of action.

"How brave," the woman whispered, unswayed by his deliberately short and uninspiring reply.

"Lots of men were brave," Alex replied gruffly, wishing to close down the conversation topic, "And lots of them didn't return. I am lucky that I did. Now tell me Miss, what exactly are you doing alone in a room that is, quite clearly, marked as being private?"

His sudden change of tact left the girl flushing red with embarrassment. He almost regretted the harshness of his words, though the pink stain which made her cheeks glow, acted like a reward for his poor manners. In truth, usually, his actions were always the height of chivalry, but this girl - whatever her name was - was setting his nerves on edge.

"I was looking for a place to freshen up," she stuttered, avoiding his eyes as she alluded to that most private of feminine acts, "And Lord Payne sent me in this direction. I think he might have been confused…"

"…By what types of pots were in the pottery room," Alex finished her sentence with a guffaw of laughter. Lord Payne, who was heir to the Ducal seat of Hawkfield was a character Alex knew well from the clubs, as well as the papers. He was renowned for his pranks and high-jinks, Alex wouldn't put it past the blighter to have sent the girl the wrong way for his own amusement.

"I'm afraid that Lord Payne was mistaken in his direction, Miss —"

"Bowstock," the girl supplied, after an oddly lengthy pause.

"Miss Bowstock," Alex felt a stab of satisfaction at having spoken her name. Remembering his manners, he gave a curt bow before introducing himself, "I am Lord Delaney."

"I know, my Lord," Miss Bowstock responded, dipping her knees in a curtsy that would not have looked out of place in any ballroom across the country. Perhaps she was gently born, Alex thought, and had simply taken up a paid position out of necessity. It was not unheard of, for many a family had lost their fortune at the hands of a bad heir.

"Allow me to escort you back to the auditorium to Miss Deveraux - I'm sure she is wondering where you have got to." Alex said and gallantly held out his arm for Miss Bowstock to take. Most women in her position would have clung on to it, enchanted by his wealth, his title and his status as a widower - but not Miss Bowstock. Instead she gave him a rather alarmed look, as though he had offered her a hissing snake and not his arm.

"Thank you," she said in a decidedly firm voice, "You're very kind, but that's really not necessary. I will find my own way back to the auditorium."

"Oh, but I insist," Alex replied, adopting his most haughty, commanding tone. He was not used to people rejecting anything that he offered - especially not women. It rankled slightly at his pride that Miss Bowstock seemed most eager to be rid of him. "I would not like anything untoward to happen to you…again."

"You are too kind," Miss Bowstock sounded pained by the kindness she referred to, "But I am afraid that I will have to insist. You have helped me far too much already, my Lord. I will find my own way back - safely - thank you."

"Are you always this stubborn?" Alex sighed irritably as he realised that she would not budge. He was not usually quick to anger, but his nerves had already been frayed by the tension of touching Miss Bowstock's hair - and now, at her seeming indifference to him, his normally ice-cool demeanour had disappeared.

"No," Miss Bowstock frowned at his words, "Are you always this bossy?"

"Yes," Alex's eyes narrowed dangerously; he was not used to insubordination of any kind. "Though I like to think I am more suggestive, than bossy *per se*."

"You're not being suggestive if what you suggest is not optional," Miss Bowstock pointed out cheerfully, "I think the word is dictatorial, my Lord. Thank you again for your kind offer, but I cannot allow you to escort me back to Miss Deveraux, for she would wonder what we had been doing together all this time…alone."

Dash it, the girl was right. Alex frowned, he may have been a man who liked reason, but he didn't like it when it was used against him.

"You win this battle, Miss Bowstock," he finally said, his eyes holding her gaze.

"Well, there won't be any other battles, my Lord," she smiled, a triumphant grin on her face, which made her eyes crinkle at the corners. "So I suppose you might say that I have won the war."

With a wave of her fingers, Miss Bowstock turned on her heel and fled the room, seemingly desperate to be free of his company. Alex stood still for a few minutes, after she had closed the door and contemplated their brief encounter. It had been a long time since he had met a woman who piqued his interest so and, unlike Miss Bowstock, he was certain that there would be many battles ahead. He was certain, because he would instigate them.

Alex reached into the breast pocket of his coat, took out his time piece and checked the hour; the afternoon had all but disappeared. Knowing that he would get no more work done that day, he decided to return home to wash and change for dinner - after which he would pay a visit to White's and reacquaint himself with Lord Deveraux. He had never been particularly fond of the chap - but it stood to reason that to be friends with the man who employed Miss Bowstock, could only be in his interest. And there was nothing that Alexander Jack de Pfeffel Delaney liked more than reason…

3 CHAPTER THREE

Hestia felt giddy for days after her encounter with the Marquess of Falconbridge. Her nerves hummed and thrummed as she carried out her daily duties and she thought that perhaps, if she had someone to confide in, that the feeling would leave her, but alas she did not have anyone to share her secret with.

Her relationship with Jane, while close, was not so close that Hestia would dare to overstep the invisible boundaries laid down by her station. As for the other staff in the household, well that was another matter entirely. Her position meant that while she was, essentially, a servant, the other servants did not view her that way. They were slightly suspicious of her, because of her closeness to the Mistress of the house, and because of this they kept their distance. Hestia, who had had a small circle of friends in Cornwall, had felt desperately lonely since her arrival in London, and now she felt even more so as she longed to discuss the dark and handsome Marquess who had spent an agonising few minutes running his hands through her hair.

Thank goodness for Henry, the King Charles Cavalier that Lady Bedford had insisted she take with her to keep her company. Henry followed her everywhere like a shadow, even sleeping at the foot of the bed in her narrow room on the top floor. When she was not required to accompany Jane out, Hestia often took the excitable dog to Green Park, where he could happily run around the wide, open fields to his heart's content.

That morning Jane had left the house early, accompanied by her wretched sister-in-law Emily. The two were gone to Hawkfield House, in St James' Square, to call on the Duchess of Hawkfield. Much to everyone's surprise, Jane and Lord Payne, had announced that they were to be married a few days previously. Hestia was thrilled for her friend, who she knew was ridiculed by her brother and his new wife for being a spinster, at having won the heart of London's most eligible bachelor. She was also thrilled because the fuss around Jane's engagement meant that Hestia had more free time to explore London.

The fashionable streets around the Deveraux's Berkeley Square home held little appeal for Hestia, who was slightly intimidated by the grand gentlemen and elegant ladies who paraded by. Instead she found herself pulled toward Green Park, where wide open fields filled with cows who grazed the grass, reminded her of home.

That morning she wandered off the path of the Queen's Walk and settled herself under a tree, allowing Henry to gambol about in the long grass before her. She settled the book she had brought with her onto her lap, turned it open to the first page, and promptly fell into a daydream — a daydream which featured a man who looked remarkably like the Marquess of Falconbridge.

"Stop. Stop. Stop." She whispered aloud, once she realised what she was doing. Had she learned nothing from her mother? Men, especially darkly, handsome ones like the Marquess, brought nothing but trouble —and Lord Delaney had already proven himself to be more than troublesome. She should have more sense than to fantasise about a man like he; a pompous, overbearing, bossy —

"I thought I recognised that bonnet."

A shadow fell over the pages of her book and Hestia looked up to see that the very man she had been inwardly insulting towering above her.

"My Lord," she stuttered, after a moment of shocked silence. "What are you doing here?"

"I might ask you the same thing."

Lord Delaney folded his arms across his chest and glared down at her, his handsome face a picture of annoyance. Confused by his anger, Hestia glanced left and right of the tree she sat under, searching for something that said she should not be there, but seeing nothing she simply replied; "I am reading, my Lord, as you can see."

"Yes, I see," the Marquess's words were like ice, matching the glacial blue of his eyes. "Reading. Alone. In Green Park."

Hestia felt as if she was missing the vital piece of information that was making the Marquess so irate. True, she was reading a book in the park, but where was the crime in that?

"Yes," she picked up the book, "It's a rather good book actually, if you don't mind I'd like to finish it."

She knew that she was being rude, and she was certain that she should not speak to a man of such high rank as the Marquess in so impertinent a manner, but so as to avoid his smouldering gaze she returned her eyes to the page.

"I do mind."

The book was plucked from her grasp, forcing her to look upward at the man who had so rudely stolen it. "In fact, I mind very much. Green Park is no place for a lady to be alone. It is dangerous."

"Dangerous?"

As though to underscore the ridiculousness of his statement, Henry, tail wagging, came bounding over toward them in keen pursuit of a butterfly. Both Hestia and the Marquess watched silently as the Cavalier gave up his chase of the colourful insect and lay down lazily in the grass, which was littered with cheerful looking daisies and cowslips. Hestia tried to hide her delight as a small tinge of pink coloured Falconbridge's cheeks as he registered that the unfolding scene had completely contradicted what he had just said. His embarrassment would almost have been endearing, if the man himself hadn't been so intimidating.

Lord Delaney was over six foot tall, with broad shoulders, muscular legs and an athletic frame that was encased in the most impeccable, fashionable attire. Attire that Hestia estimated probably cost many times more than her yearly wage. All this would have been tolerable if it were not for his face, which was so sinfully handsome it was almost painful to look at. He was all hard angles —high cheekbones and a strong jaw —but they were softened somewhat by his eyes—a startling blue framed by black lashes— as well as his hair which was dark, with a slight curl. He reminded Hestia somewhat of the paintings of angels one saw in the galleries in town, and she could see why the papers had dubbed him The Marquess of Temptation, for everything about him was tempting and lush.

"Yes," the Marquess continued, his jaw set stubbornly, "Despite appearances, Green Park can be a hotbed for criminal activity. I won't rest easy until I see you safely home. I could not bear the thought of a lady, such as yourself, coming to any harm."

"But I am not a lady," Hestia gently reminded him, her thoughts flashing to the newspaper article on her father. She was the daughter of a privateer, born out of scandal, she was the furthest thing possible from a lady.

"Says who?"

The Marquess quirked an eyebrow, an act that seemed to let loose a colony of butterflies in Hestia's stomach.

"Says everyone," she laughed nervously, standing to her feet. "Society, Lady Jarvis; why if the patronesses of Almack's were to interview me, they would say it too. I am no Lady, my Lord, though I am a Lady's companion and that is good enough for me."

She gave a light laugh, trying to brush off the awkwardness of the conversation —why, oh why, had she not simply ignored his initial remark? Now he was staring at her thoughtfully, in a way that made her feel ridiculously thrilled and overwhelmingly nervous, all at the same time.

"You are every inch the lady, Miss Bowstock," he finally replied solemnly. He hesitated, as though he wanted to say more, but looked down at Henry instead. "Though this little chap is no gentleman."

Indeed, during the course of their conversation, Henry had decided that the Marquess's gleaming Hessians looked good enough to eat. The small dog was licking them with great determination, as though sensing that at one stage in their lifetime, the boots had previously been an edible animal.

"Oh, Henry," Hestia gave a sigh, and scooped the small offender up into her arms. "You must not lick the Marquess's boots, it's naughty."

"Does he respond well to verbal reasoning?" there was a note of amusement in Lord Delaney's voice that made the corners of Hestia's lips tug into an involuntary smile.

"He does not," she grinned, "Henry only responds to bribes. Food is his first preference, affection comes in a close second."

"Then he is like every other man in the world."

For a few seconds they both stood in the tall grass, grinning stupidly at each other. Hestia, who had never spent any time alone with a man, wondered if this would be considered flirting.

How wrong I was about him, she thought with surprise, annoyed with herself for having misjudged him so.

"Enough chit chat," the Marquess's tone was suddenly brusque, "As I was saying Green Park is no place for a woman to be alone. Come, I will take you back to Berkeley Square."

"And as I was saying, I have no need to be escorted anywhere, my Lord," Hestia bristled at his tone, her affectionate thoughts evaporating as he once again assumed the air of an entitled Lord. "You would do me more harm than good escorting me home, how would I explain your presence if anyone from the household saw you?"

"I hope someone sees me," Falconbridge drawled, "For I want to have words with Miss Deveraux on her lack of concern for your safety."

Never before had Hestia felt so overwhelmed with frustration; it was like conversing with a brick wall. A stubborn headed, arrogant, pompous brick wall. She knew that no matter what she said, the Marquess would not listen, so, sensing she had no other choice, she turned on her heel and began to stalk away.

"Where are you going?"

Hestia ignored his irritated call and continued on her path across the field. Henry, who was still in her arms, wriggled in a valiant attempt to escape her clutches and return to the Marquess —but she held tight. She did not once look over her shoulder to see if the Marquess was following her, but she knew that he was from the annoyed sighs she heard as he shadowed her steps. When she reached the Queen's Walk, a stone path that ran the length of the park, she saw a huge, dark stallion tethered to the gate post. From its impressive gleaming coat and its sheer magnificence, Hestia assumed that the horse belonged to Lord Delaney. She did not wait for him to untie the beast, instead she continued on with great determination —she would reach Berkeley Square without the Marquess's assistance.

She crossed at Piccadilly, weaving her way through the carriages and carts that thronged the street with Henry still in her arms. Mayfair was a short stroll away, Hestia hurried along the much quieter Clarges Street, where finally she dared to look behind her. He was gone; she breathed a sigh of relief. He must have lost sight of her at Piccadilly — thank goodness for that. She set Henry down on the footpath and as she did so realised that she had left her book behind her in the park.

Drat, she thought with annoyance. The book, a small leather-bound volume, had detailed Napoleon's exploits in Egypt at the start of the century and his surrender of Cairo to the English. It wasn't her usual reading material, but Jane had told her that it delved into the disappearance of several ancient artifacts during the military transition, artifacts that were thought to have been stolen from the Navy by pirates.

Instantly Hestia's mind had leapt to the newspaper article on her father, and how he was supposed to have carried out daring raids on Navy ships at that time. Truthfully, the book had been rather a bore, filled with analysis of military tactics and it had not mentioned her father once, but it had reignited her zeal for finding out what had happened to him that fateful night.

She glanced back toward Piccadilly, thinking that she might return to the park to collect the novel, but her eyes caught a glimpse of a tall man on horseback at the far end of the road.

Drat him anyway, she sighed, picking Henry back up and hurrying toward home; it would have to wait for another day.

4 CHAPTER FOUR

He was losing his mind.

That was the only explanation that Alex could think of for his uncharacteristic behaviour that morning. Whilst riding through Green Park, he had caught sight of a most familiar looking bonnet and, on impulse, had dismounted his horse and followed the bonnet's wearer across the fields. He had then proceeded to be so overcome with righteous indignation at the object of his affection's irresponsible behaviour that he had failed in his initial mission - to charm Miss Belinda Bowstock.

Judging by the angry, stiff set of shoulders that he was trailing through the streets of Mayfair, his charm needed more than a little polishing; Miss Bowstock was livid with anger. Alex kept a safe distance as she turned onto Berkeley Square, watching to make sure she was safely inside Jarvis House, before turning back in the direction of Piccadilly.

Why he was so fixated with Miss Bowstock was beyond his understanding, and Alex hated anything that could not be rationally explained. She was the opposite of the type of woman he preferred; where his usual paramours were sultry and experienced, Miss Bowstock was innocent and more than a little naive. Not to mention stubborn headed. Alex, given his title, was used to women veritably throwing themselves at him —not stalking away in the opposite direction without so much as a backward glance.

The streets of London were thronged with people, rich and poor, going about their daily business. Alex guided Pegasus carefully through the heavy morning traffic of carriages and carts, finally reaching his original destination about a half hour after he had planned.

The offices of Miley and Son Solicitors was located on Half Moon Street, which itself was named after the tavern that stood on the corner. The buildings were modest yet genteel, with brown brick facades and sash windows that revealed little of the occupants inside. Miley and Sons was located two doors up from the tavern, with only a small brass plaque beside the front door to announce its presence.

Alex knocked, a loud rap, that was instantly answered by a beleaguered looking young man with sandy hair and spectacles.

"My Lord," the young man gave an exaggerated bow, "We have been waiting for your arrival. Old Miley cannot begin reading the will until all beneficiaries are present."

"My apologies for being late," Alex replied, feeling not in the least bit sorry for his tardiness. He had no idea why he had been summoned to the reading of his late wife's, late cousin's husband's will, and if it weren't for the fact that Mr. Miley Senior had sent him no less than five letters demanding his presence, Alex would not have come at all.

"No need to apologise," the young man blustered, gesturing for Alex to follow him down a dim corridor. "There is no hurry, Mr Miley Senior abhors rushing of any kind."

Nearly half an hour later, as Alex waited for the elderly, consumptive solicitor to finish reading the last will and testament of David Stockbow, he realised that the young man had been right. Old Miley spoke at a pace that left Alex stifling a yawn as he waited for him to finish. A young man named Captain Black, the only other person present, wore a similar look of boredom as he listened to the old man ramble on.

"Ah," Miley rasped, the phlegm in his chest audibly gurgling, "Now we get to the good bit."

Alex perked up, his interest piqued. David Stockbow had been a notorious privateer in his younger days, and was suspected of having stolen many things, including ancient Egyptian artifacts, among which, it was thought, was the missing part of the Egyptian steele he and Pierre Dubois were trying to decipher. Was it possible that Stockbow had learned of their familial connection and Alex's passion for hieroglyphics and decided to do the honest thing? Alex doubted it, but he pricked his ears and listened intently none the less.

"To my daughter, Hestia B. Stockbow, I bequest all my worldly goods, excepting my ruby-hilt sword which I leave to Captain James Black, as thanks for saving my life."

Alex stole a glance at the young man who sat to the left of him; he was well dressed and handsome, not the type of man who looked like he would be anyway inclined toward saving a criminal's life. He idly wondered how on earth that scenario had arisen, but his imaginings were cut off as the solicitor spoke again.

"And finally," Miley read slowly, his rheumy blue eyes fixed on Alex, "Should I die before my daughter reaches her majority, I wish to entrust her guardianship to Alex Delaney, Marquess of Falconbridge."

"A ward?" Alex was so shocked he had not realised he had spoken aloud until Miley replied "Yes" with a cackle.

"Good God," Alex blustered, "What on earth am I supposed to do with a ward?"

"Well," Miley lay down the sheath of paper on the table and eyed him with unconcealed amusement, "You could start by finding her first. You see, since her father's death, Miss Hestia B. Stockbow seems to have disappeared off the face of the earth."

It took all of Alex's will power not to snarl in annoyance, for the elderly solicitor looked positively gleeful as he imparted the news. Wonderful, Alex thought to himself, not only had he inherited a ward, he had inherited a mystery as well.

"I can help you find her," Captain Black spoke for the first time, his voice as clipped and aristocratic as Alex's own. "For I owe Stockbow my life as much as he owes his to me."

The offer to trade the gallant Captain his ward for the Captain's ruby sword was on the tip of Alex's tongue, but he somehow resisted.

"Thank you Captain," he said instead. "Once Miley furnishes me with the last known whereabouts of Miss Stockbow perhaps we shall retire to the Half Moon to discuss our search?"

"I could do with a glass of ale," Black replied cheerfully.

"I could do with a gallon of it," was Alex's dour response.

White's was not a place that Alex frequented regularly; he was usually too absorbed in his work to bother dedicating himself to nights of drinking, like so many of his peers. That evening, however, after having spent the afternoon in the rather amicable company of Captain Black, Alex found himself alighting the steps of the prestigious gentleman's club for the first time that season.

"Lud," a cheerful voice called as he entered the warmly lit drawing room. "Falconbridge, I haven't seen you in an age."

"Payne," Alex inclined his head toward James Fairweather, whom he had known since childhood, "Fancy meeting you here."

Lord Payne either missed or ignored the sarcasm in Alex's tone, for he gestured for the Marquess to join him at his table at the club's famous bow window.

"My congratulations on your engagement," Alex offered, as a discreet footman placed a fresh decanter of brandy before the two men. "Miss Deveraux is quite the woman, rather different from the wife I had imagined you would choose."

"I know," Payne looked very pleased with himself, "She's terribly clever. Lud knows what she sees in a man like me."

Alex, if he hadn't known that Payne was a most loyal and kind man, would have been inclined to agree. The younger man had always been known as a rakehall, who was forever involved in some sort of trouble, brought on by his impulsive nature. That he had chosen the sensible Miss Deveraux as his bride had shocked the ton, though judging by the smitten look on Payne's face, it was a most suitable match.

"To your future health and happiness," Alex said, raising the tumbler of brandy that had been poured for him. He drank deeply on the amber liquid, savouring the warmth of it trickling into his belly. A man could get fond of brandy, he mused, if he put his mind to it.

"How goes all in the world of..." Lord Payne trailed off and threw Alex an apologetic glance.

"Hieroglyphics," he helpfully supplied, suppressing a grin. "It does not go well, I'm afraid. Dubois and I are trying to translate a piece of writing on a stone steele, but a chunk of it is missing, which is making the whole exercise rather pointless."

"Well, couldn't you just try find the missing chunk?" Payne asked, wearing a patient expression on his handsome face.

"Gosh, I don't know why we didn't think of that."

Alex's father had once told him that sarcasm was the lowest form of humour and when Payne gave him a pitying smile, Alex began to see why. His scoffing tone had gone un-noted by Lord Payne, who grinned brilliantly at having solved Alex's dilemma.

"Sometimes we overlook the most obvious solution," Payne said, lifting his glass in a toast to simplicity. Alex did not know whether to laugh or cry and in the end he simply opted to raise his own glass in a return toast.

"Yes, well, I'm afraid I won't get around to searching for the stone anytime soon," Alex said with a sigh, "I'm headed to Cornwall in the morning."

"Bit chilly for the seaside, old chap."

"Would that I was going to the seaside," Alex laughed, "I have...a legal matter to attend to."

He didn't want to mention the business with Miss Hestia Stockbow in front of Payne, lest the chap said something to his intended, who might then mention it to her companion. Goodness, he started as his train of thought reached its end, why on earth was he concerned about what Miss Belinda Bowstock thought of his having inherited a ward? As the Marquess of Falconbridge he was one of the wealthiest men in England and, with that, came power and influence. He shouldn't care about the thoughts of a lowly lady's companion —and yet he did.

"Sounds exciting," Payne deadpanned, setting his empty tumbler on the table and standing up. "If you can bear any more excitement when you get back, come down to Hawkfield Manor. Caroline is talking about holding a small get together of friends and family before the wedding."

"Sounds a treat," Alex answered truthfully, for his mind had instantly deduced that the chances of Miss Bowstock being present were quite high. He lifted his hand in a lazy wave as Lord Payne made his exit. The club was quiet, as it was midweek, and only a few souls still loitered in the drawing room. From inside the breast pocket of his coat Alex withdrew the book that Miss Bowstock had left behind in Green Park. It was a small, leather-bound work on military tactics and battles, focusing especially on the period that the French occupied Egypt, some twenty years previously. Alex was rather bewildered by Miss Bowstock's choice of reading material; he had expected it to be a Gothic Romance, which were popular with the young ladies of the ton. That she read obscure writings on what had been, for the most part, unimportant military skirmishes just added to her intrigue. He could not place what it was about Miss Bowstock that had so captured his interest; yes, she was beautiful, but so were many other women - women with better social standing than she. Perhaps it was that she seemed thoroughly unimpressed by his title, where most people saw nothing but his rank when they saw him. It was that, he decided, and her fragility, because, while Miss Bowstock did her best to give the impression of being thoroughly independent and self-reliant, Alex saw past her stubborn exterior. She seemed to be completely and utterly alone in the world and it inspired feelings of tender protectiveness that he had never felt toward anyone before...even if she was loathe to take the protection he offered. He heaved a sigh and finished his drink; his protective feelings toward Miss Bowstock would have to be put on hold, for he had a missing ward to find.

5 CHAPTER FIVE

Hestia had never seen a house as splendid as Hawkfield Manor. True, in Truro, Lord and Lady Bedford had lived in one of the finest homes in the locality, but the seat of the Baronage paled in comparison to the Ducal seat of Hawkfield. Hestia counted fifteen bay windows as the carriage trundled up the drive, before she lost count and gave up. She could feel the disapproving eyes of the Viscountess Jarvis on her and hastily she sat back in her seat, attempting to quell the obvious look of awe on her face.

The carriage journey from London, while relatively short, had been most arduous, mostly because of the Viscount and Viscountess. Jane's brother had a nasty habit of disparaging Jane's every word, thought and movement, and his new wife was no better. Hestia had been forced to bite her tongue several times over the few hours that they were all crammed together in the carriage's compartment and to say that she was relieved that the journey was at an end was an understatement.

Two liveried footmen rushed to meet them as they drew up at the sweeping front steps of the manor. Hestia was the last to alight the vehicle and she lagged slightly behind the Deverauxs as they entered, so that she could take in the sight of the Ducal seat without the disapproving eyes of the Viscountess watching her. It took all of her will power not to cry out "Lud" as she took in the double-height ceiling of the entrance hall with its stained glass dome that shed dappled light onto the marble tiles. The hall was bigger than most houses; Hestia counted at least a dozen marble pillars, which led to the grand, sweep of the staircase.

"Welcome, welcome," Lady Caroline, who was Lord Payne's sister called to the group. Her husband, a rather quiet man, stood beside her, a warm smile on his intelligent face.

"How was the journey?" Lady Caroline enquired politely.

"Arduous," Lady Deveraux cried with a heavy sigh. To be fair to her,

Hestia thought with alarm, the Viscountess was looking slightly green around the gills after the carriage ride. She watched quietly as Lady Caroline summoned a maid to take Lord and Lady Jarvis to their suite of rooms, a little relieved that she would soon not have to suffer their company. Once they had departed, Lady Caroline, who was petite and almost bird like, gave Jane a warm hug. The two women began talking about the guests who were due to arrive, allowing Hestia the opportunity to take in the beauty of the hall. Dozens of portraits of hung on the walls, all of the previous Dukes of Hawkfield and their families. Hestia was delighted by the detail of the pictures and how the fashions changed drastically in each different portrait; it was almost like seeing a timeline of the history of England. She allowed her mind to wander, thinking on the lives that the previous Dukes must have led, only coming out of her reverie when she heard Lady Caroline exclaim, "Why the Marquess of Falconbridge, of course. He and James have been friends since childhood."

Falconbridge?

Hestia felt her face flame red at the mention of the name of the man who had permeated her every thought since that morning in Green Park. Every day since she had scanned the society pages in the newspaper, hoping for a glimpse into what ball he might have attended, or if he was seen out riding on The Mile in Hyde Park, but her searches had yielded nothing. Lord Delaney was quite the mystery; all that Hestia knew of him was that he was a widower, and that fact had been gleaned from eavesdropping on one of Lady Jarvis's morning callers. The caller, a Miss Shufflebotham had been bemoaning the lack of eligible bachelors that season.

"The only good one left is Lord Delaney," she had huffed, unaware that Hestia, who was sitting in the corner, had stilled at the mention of his name. "But he is never seen out. Some say he's still mourning his late wife, though my father says he's more interested in dead languages than dead wives."

This barb had earned a cackle from Lady Jarvis, before the two women carried on their inane gossiping.

Now the Marquess was expected here and he would sleep under the same roof as her. Hestia felt clammy at the very thought of having to spend any time near him; while she found him dreadfully attractive, she also found him mildly terrifying. Not to mention haughty, rude and inappropriately overbearing for a man who could claim no connection to her.

"Oh look," Lady Caroline called, glancing out the open doorway, "Here they are now."

Indeed, as she spoke, Lord Delaney and Lord Payne were just reaching the top of the driveway, both men having opted to travel on horseback. Lord Payne's hair was tousled from the ride, and his clothes were slightly rumpled, whereas Lord Delaney was immaculate. Hestia watched surreptitiously as he dismounted his steed, handing the reins to a waiting footman. His clothes were pristine; he wore a dark riding coat over buckskin breeches that were tucked into a pair of gleaming, black Hessians. She felt Henry, who was seated at her feet, perk up at the sight of the familiar figure.

"Oh, no you don't," she whispered, scooping the mischievous dog into her arms and stealing away behind a pillar where she hoped she might not be noted by the Marquess. From her vantage point she watched as the two men strode into the hall to greet Lady Caroline and Jane. Lord Payne's face was creased in a warm smile and his every movement was ebullient, while the Marquess was much more reserved, his expression stiff and haughty. Lady Caroline fussed about the pair and called for the housekeeper, Mrs Hughes, to come take Jane and Hestia to their rooms.

"Put Miss Bowstock in the Lavender Room," she instructed the older woman, then turned to glance around the hall, her face a picture of confusion. "Where has she gone?"

"I'm here," Hestia whispered, coming out from behind the pillar, still clutching a struggling Henry in her arms. She kept her eyes focused on Jane and Lady Caroline, too afraid to glance at the towering figure of the Marquess to her right. Jane's eyes narrowed in thought as she surveyed Hestia, glancing at the Marquess then back at her companion.

"Come Belinda," she said kindly, as a footman took their bags and Mrs Hughes began to lead the way to their suite of rooms. Hestia trailed the group as they slowly made their way up the stairs, feeling very conscious that a set of blue eyes might be following her. The urge to look over her shoulder was too tempting to resist and the instant that she did, her eyes locked with those of Lord Delaney. His smouldering gaze knocked the wind out of her and she immediately turned her head away, wondering if he could hear her heartbeat, which thundered like a storm in her chest.

"I cannot go to dinner Jane, I have a terrible migraine."

It was half true; Hestia's head did ache after the journey but it was not so bad that she would not have been able to eat. In truth, she was famished, but the thought of sitting opposite Lord Delaney through five courses was too difficult to contemplate.

"Oh, Belinda. It's not because of the Marquess, is it?"

It still felt strange to Hestia to be referred to as Belinda and it took her a moment to respond to Jane, who was seated at the window of the small sitting room which joined their two bedrooms together.

"It's not, I promise," Hestia replied firmly, her eyes wide as she tried to convey her innocence. "It's just that the journey has left me a little fatigued. Even Lady Jarvis is tired after it, and you know how much she loves to socialise."

The Viscountess had cried off attending dinner, an act that had left Jane worried, for like Hestia she had noted Lady Jarvis's pallid complexion earlier.

"As long as you're not going hungry simply so you don't have to see him," Jane replied kindly, "I shan't let him chastise you ever again."

Hestia felt a little guilty at Jane's fiercely protective words. When they had reached their rooms earlier Jane had immediately begun to question Hestia on what had transpired between her and the Marquess, to make both of them look so uncomfortable in each other's presence. Hestia had fibbed and told Jane that Falconbridge had berated her for touching one of the artifacts at Montagu House, which was almost true. Jane had been incensed on her behalf, leaving Hestia feeling a little worried that her mistress might take the Marquess to task over it all.

"Honestly, Jane," Hestia protested weakly, "It's just a migraine. It has nothing to do with Lord Delaney and I pray that you will say nothing to him. It's all forgotten about —I swear."

"If you say so," Jane sighed, placing the book she had been holding in her lap aside, "I'd best head down, lest they send out a search party for me."

In truth, it was rather early to be going down for dinner, but Jane was harbouring secrets of her own. Her old paramour, an entomologist by the name of Mr Jackson had reappeared from South America. Hestia wasn't overly fond of Mr Jackson, who was pompous and rather dry, but Jane had revealed that her engagement to Lord Payne was nothing more than a ruse to placate the Duke, who was threatening to cut Lord Payne off from his allowance. It was all very complex, Hestia thought, and she secretly believed that while Jane thought the engagement was merely an act, Lord Payne disagreed. It was clear to even the most casual observer that the Hawkfield heir was head over heels in love with Miss Deveraux.

Love -there was that word again. Her mother had been right, Hestia thought as she waved Jane away, love brought nothing but trouble.

Once Jane had left, Hestia wandered into her bedroom, the aptly titled Lavender Room. The walls were covered with wallpaper that was patterned with little sprigs of the plant, and the bedsheets were a dusty lilac colour. Hestia threw herself down on the bed with a happy sigh, glad for the opportunity to relax her aching muscles. She must have fallen asleep, for she opened her eyes —what felt like only moments later— to find the room in darkness. A loud rumbling filled the room and it took Hestia a second to realise that it was her stomach - she was famished. For a few minutes she debated whether to get up and see if there were any staff still in the kitchen that she might beg for a slice of bread, until another loud rumble decided her.

"I'll wake the whole house if I don't," she reasoned, as she slipped out into the dark hallway. Luckily she had been too exhausted to undress, so she did not mind the chill of the night air. Hawkfield Manor was enormous - Hestia found her way back to the main entrance hall, but from there was unsure what direction to take.

"The kitchens are always at the back of the house," she thought, deciding to take corridor to her right, which looked promising enough. There was not a soul to be seen in the dark hallway, leaving Hestia to wonder what time it was. Judging by the echoing silence of the house, it was well after midnight and everyone —staff included—was in bed.

The hallway became less grand as she walked down it, and at the end she turned a corner and found the kitchens. A low fire still burned in the grate, illuminating the enormous room which was lined with shelves stuffed full of crockery and cooking utensils. A set of doors toward the back of the room led to the pantry, where Hestia gratefully stole some dry bread and a small lump of cheese. She was hungrily swallowing her makeshift sandwich, when a low, droll voice spoke, startling her.

"You wouldn't be so hungry if you hadn't skipped dinner."

Hestia turned and found the Marquess of Falconbridge standing behind her, his face a picture of amusement. He was undressed, well as undressed as Hestia had ever seen him, his shirt sleeves rolled up and his cravat removed, revealing a tantalising glimpse of tanned skin.

"I didn't skip dinner," she whispered waspishly once she had swallowed the chunk of bread in her mouth. "I had a migraine."

The Marquess did not reply, merely raised his eyebrows in a condescending manner that implied he thought her lying.

"Oh," Hestia growled, "You are insufferably conceited if you think that I avoided dinner just because of you."

"Did I say that?" Falconbridge's eyes were dancing with laughter, a smile tugging at the corner of his lips. "I wasn't aware that I had spoken at all."

"You didn't speak," Hestia agreed, feeling flustered at his cool composure. Her own cheeks were staining red, both from his cool, arrogance and the almost insolent way his eyes watched her. "But, then you didn't need to speak, for your expression said it all."

"I do apologise," he replied, though he sounded anything but sorry, "I shall have to make sure that my facial muscles remain completely impassive in your company, lest I offend you."

"You don't offend me," Hestia, who felt completely out of her depth protested, "You—you—you—"

Lord Delaney remained silently watching her as she trailed off, unable to put into words what it was that he made her feel. The expression of amusement in his eyes was replaced by one of kindness and he reached out a hand to gently touch her arm.

"Come," he said patiently, "You shouldn't be out of bed at this hour — thank goodness it was I who found you and not a groom or some other man with unsavoury intentions."

Hestia wanted to reply, she wanted to ask him why it was that he was out wandering the halls of Hawkfield Manor in the middle of the night, but the touch of his skin against her bare arm had left her breathless and she was unable to speak. She followed the Marquess as he led her down the hallway to the entrance hall, where he left her at the bottom step of the staircase.

"I trust you will find your way from here," he said with a curt bow.

"I will. Thank you, my Lord," she responded stiffly, her mind exhausted from the late hour and the torrent of emotions that were pouring through her. She turned from him and began to slowly climb the stairs, only pausing at the sound of his voice.

"Miss Bowstock?" he called and when she turned she saw that he was smiling. "I hope that I will see you at breakfast in the morning. You are far too thin as it is, I won't stand for you skipping meals."

"You won't stand?" Hestia could feel her ire rising again, but then she saw that he was laughing and she knew that he was deliberately trying to rise her.

"Goodnight, my Lord," she said firmly, trying to resist the smile that was threatening to crack her cool exterior. She did not wait to hear his reply, instead she turned and hurried up the staircase, feeling so light that she almost thought she had grown wings.

6 CHAPTER SIX

When Alex awoke the next morning he was filled with a sense of restless energy that he knew could only be subdued by exercise. His mind slipped back to the image of Belinda Bowstock standing in the kitchen, her eyes sparking with indignation and he revised his decision —he would have to engage in some very vigorous exercise to quell the energy that filled him.

As usual he had woken at dawn and the solitary groom in Hawkfield's stables rubbed sleep from his eyes as he saddled up the Marquess's horse. The countryside around the estate was typical of Surrey; lush, rolling green fields, dotted with the occasional yellow brick farm house. Alex pushed Pegasus harder than usual, relishing the aching in his muscles as the stallion tore across the open fields. His mind was still on Belinda and her innocent beauty but his conscience was niggling at him, urging him to think instead on his responsibilities. Namely Miss Hestia B. Stockbow who, following her father's death, seemed to have disappeared completely.

Alex's trip to Truro had yielded few clues. The villagers had pointed him in the direction of Lady Bedford, a tight-lipped old dame, who claimed to know nothing about what had become of Miss Stockbow.

"She simply disappeared," Lady Bedford had insisted, stroking the ears of the elderly Cavalier in her lap. "I wouldn't blame her for wishing to make a fresh start after all the scandal her father caused, would you, Lord Delaney?"

Alex started at the mention of his name, for the sight of the small King Charles had reminded him of Miss Bowstock which had sent him into a most un-masculine daydream.

"If Miss Stockbow wishes to disappear to preserve her reputation," Alex had eventually replied, "Then that is her prerogative. As her guardian, however, my prerogative is to ensure that wherever she is she is safe and financially secure. If you happen to come across her Lady Bedford, do send her in my direction."

He had returned to London after that, certain that Lady Bedford knew where this Hestia Stockbow was hiding and that the old woman was sensible enough to let the girl know there were funds available for her. If that failed, Captain Black, who had business to attend to in Cornwall, had promised to keep his eyes and ears peeled for any hint of the young woman. The sun had risen fully by the time that Alex returned to Hawkfield Manor. He bathed quickly, changed into fresh clothes and made his way down to the dining room, where a buffet breakfast was being served.

The only people present when he arrived were Mr Jackson, the dull entomologist and Lady Caroline, who looked much relieved at his arrival.

"There you are Falconbridge," she exclaimed, patting the seat next to her. "I was beginning to think that all my guests would be abed until after midday."

"Frightful waste of time, sleeping," Mr Jackson muttered, wiping his mouth with a serviette. "Excuse me Lady Caroline, Lord Delaney. The Duke has kindly offered me the use of his library and I cannot waste such an opportunity."

"Oh, don't stay on our account," Caroline waved the spectacled man away, her dark eyes dancing with mischief. Alex fetched himself a plate of eggs and kippers and took a seat beside Caroline, who was sipping on milky tea.

"Tell me," she said, placing her cup down and glancing at him fondly. "How have you been Alex? I said to Giles only yesterday that it felt like I had not seen you in years, and he reminded me that was because it has been years since we've met."

Alex chewed slowly on his forkful of fish, as he attempted to formulate a reply. He knew that Caroline, like the rest of the ton, thought him mad with grief since his wife's death, but in truth he had not been. His marriage to Amelia had been hasty, inspired by grief at his brother's death and an overwhelming feeling of duty to continue the line.

Marry in haste, repent at leisure was a phrase he had not fully understood until he and Amelia had been wed. She had transformed from a sweet, agreeable woman into a spoilt, vain, temperamental shrew the moment she could claim the title Marchioness. Alex, who had never been overly fond of the society that his new bride was obsessed by, had retreated to Montagu House, uncaring of the rumours that soon began to circulate of the new Marchioness's penchant for affairs with anyone from stable hands to members of his club.

He had made a huge mistake in marrying her; he knew this. There had never been any love between them, indeed Amelia had often looked at him with eyes full of scorn, but even with that, when she had died after a freak carriage accident in which one of her paramours was driving, he had been filled with guilt. This guilt had pushed him further into his studies of the ancient languages, to the point that it had bordered on obsession. The single-minded resolve to solve the mystery of what was written on the ancient Egyptian steele that he and Dubois were studying had consumed his every waking thought for years —until he had found Miss Belinda Bowstock, tied by a bonnet string to a Greek urn. His every waking thought was now dedicated to her, not to mention his dreams, when he did sleep, which featured her regularly. It was ridiculous, he was a man of four and thirty, he should know better than to be distracted by a pair of big, blue eyes.

"Has it been years?" he finally questioned, deliberately making his tone light. "Goodness, how quickly they pass. I suppose I have hidden myself away for quite some time, though I intend to change that."

He saw Caroline's eyebrows knit together speculatively and resisted smiling at her reaction. He knew she was wondering if he was insinuating that he wished to find a bride, but he quickly changed the topic of conversation, happy to keep her speculating, for he was not too certain of the answer himself. Yes, he knew he needed to wed, but the only woman who held his interest was wholly unsuited to being a Marchioness. It would shock society if he were to announce his intentions toward Miss Bowstock but then, he thought with a smirk, when had he ever cared about what society thought?

The afternoon activities consisted of a walk in the grounds of Hawkfield Manor, followed by a picnic by the lake. Alex had thought that perhaps, circumstances permitting, he might fall into step with Miss Bowstock and manage a few stolen words with her. Circumstances did not permit, however, because Miss Bowstock seemed determined to avoid him.

"Goodness, Belinda is full of energy," Lady Caroline noted, as Jane's companion hurtled ahead of the group. Henry, who Alex was growing rather fond of, kept pausing to look back at him, as though he wanted the Marquess to chase after him. They were nearing the lake and Alex could see that laid out under a copse of nearby trees was a large picnic for the guests. He evidently wasn't the only one to spot it, for Miss Bowstock emitted a wail of annoyance as Henry tore off in the direction of the luncheon.

"Oh, dear, she'll lose her bonnet," Jane gasped, as the group watched Belinda race after the mischievous Cavalier.

"That would hardly be a tragedy," Alex drawled, for the bonnet in question was the same hideous one from Montagu House. The group watched in awe as Jane's prediction came true and Belinda's bonnet was torn from her head by a gust of wind and carried toward the lake. She paused and turned in the direction that her hat had flown, then turned back to look at Henry who was still making his way, on his short legs, toward the picnic. Miss Bowstock obviously decided that lunch was more important than the hat for, after a pause, she continued chasing the dog. Alex heaved a sigh and made for the lake. Chivalry demanded that he rescue the hat from ruin, but he really wished Miss Bowstock had a nicer hat to rescue. The bonnet had landed in the reeds, by the lakes edge. He only had to wade in a few steps to retrieve it, but the bottom of the lake was muddy and even those few steps rendered his own boots quite ruined.

Miss Bowstock stood as he returned, her expression nervous as she took in the state of his muddied boots and breeches.

"Oh, dear," she whispered, as he neared her. "You should not have ruined your clothing for my bonnet. It is just a silly, old thing —not worth rescuing."

"Of course it was," he countered, handing her the slightly muddied hat. She took it with a curtsy and a word of thanks, then ushered him over to where the blankets were laid out, quite obviously eager to be rid of his company.

"Oh, there you are Jane," Miss Bowstock said with relief, throwing herself down on the blanket, so close to Miss Deveraux that she was almost seated in her lap. Alex glowered; he was not used to women throwing themselves away from him —quite the opposite, in fact.

He took a seat on the same blanket, beside Lord Payne, who was engaging the two women in easy, amusing conversation. Never before had Alex felt so jealous of Payne's casual charm, and when the young Lord offered to fetch a plate for Miss Bowstock, Alex nearly belted him.

"I will fetch Miss Bowstock a plate," he said stiffly, rising easily and padding across the grass to where the luncheon buffet was laid out. He took a plate, piled it high with cold meats, strawberries and radishes, and returned to where the object of his affections sat. The only problem was, that she did not wear a look of affection on her own face, in fact she looked rather like she was about to cast up her accounts.

"Eat up," he instructed, sounding much sterner than he had intended. Miss Bowstock nervously picked up a strawberry and obediently popped it into her mouth and began chewing with a pained expression. Alex had deliberately placed himself so that the bulk of his body blocked Lord Payne and Miss Deveraux from view, he was determined that he would have his few stolen moments with Miss Bowstock.

"I did not see you at breakfast," he stated simply. At his words Belinda's eyes left her plate and locked with his for the first time, leaving him almost winded with desire.

"I slept late," she offered, picking nervously at the food he had given her. "I'm usually early to rise, but last night I found it difficult to fall back asleep, after—"

Her face flamed red as she mentioned their midnight meeting. A thrill of satisfaction coursed through Alex; at least he had not been alone in finding sleep difficult after their brief encounter. Belinda's head turned as Henry padded over to them, his tail wagging as he sniffed the meat upon his mistress's plate. He rested his head on Belinda's lap, his eyes wide and innocent, as he gazed up at her, begging.

"He's not very well behaved," Alex observed, as Miss Bowstock discreetly fed the dog a small piece of ham.

"No, he's not," she agreed with a chuckle, flashing him a mischievous smile. "But I adore him, despite his obvious character flaws - he reminds me of home."

"And where is home?" Alex asked, leaning forward to hear her answer. Miss Bowstock was a complete mystery to him; he knew nothing of her lineage or her past; it was as though she had simply appeared out of thin air.

"Cornwall."

"Cornwall is rather large," Alex said, wondering if she was being deliberately vague, her answer was so curt. Did she have something to hide?

"It is," eagerly Miss Bowstock nodded her head in agreement. "Very big. Have you ever been, my Lord?"

Goodness; he would have laughed at the obviousness of her tactics had he not been so intrigued by her evasiveness.

"I have just returned from Truro," he volunteered, casually leaning over to scratch Henry's ears. The dog glanced at him dismissively, he would not pay attention to mere ear scratching, when there was food to beg for.

"What were you doing in Truro?"

Alex knew he wasn't imagining the slightly defensive note to Miss Bowstock's question and his eyes narrowed in thought. This was a woman with something to hide, and he was determined to find out what exactly it was. His inquisition was put on hold as Lord Payne let out a call for a game of cricket. Alex rose to his feet, with a short nod to Belinda, ignoring the look of relief on her face. He would have answers from her, he decided, but he would not scare her into revealing her past…he would woo her instead.

7 CHAPTER SEVEN

That evening the fable of the boy who cried wolf sprung to Hestia's mind as she suffered through dinner. Why had she pretended to have a migraine on her first night at Hawkfield Manor, when this evening the lie would have served a far greater purpose. Namely, it would have allowed her to avoid the Marquess of Falconbridge, who seemed determined to find out everything he could about her past.

He was suspicious of her, she knew, though she also knew that he could have no reason to connect her to the scandalous life and death of David Stockbow, unless she gave him one.

"We were speaking of Truro," Lord Delaney said, as he sidled up to her in the drawing room, after dinner. Tea was being served in delicate china cups, allowing Hestia a minute's relief as she pretended to be distracted by adding lumps of sugar to her drink. "And you were just about to tell me where it was that you had lived in Cornwall."

"Was that what we were speaking of, my Lord?" she finally asked gaily, hoping that Falconbridge could not hear her heart, which was beating a loud, nervous tattoo in her breast. "Oh, yes, just before you left to play cricket. Tell me, where did you learn to play so well?"

She opened her eyes in what she hoped was a wide and innocent way, crossing her fingers that the Marquess, like every other man, would jump at the opportunity to speak of his accomplishments.

"At Eton," he answered smoothly, sitting down, uninvited, on the overstuffed sofa beside her. The china cup that he held looked ridiculously small in his hand and the sheer size of him left her feeling even more nervous. All his questions would be so much easier to bear if he wasn't so intimidating looking, she thought with annoyance. It wasn't just his size that daunted her, but his face as well —he was sinfully handsome. His cheekbones were high, his mouth generous and his eyes hypnotising in their intensity —he truly was a tempting specimen of a man. A lock of Falconbridge's dark hair had fallen out of place and for a moment Hestia felt the urge to brush it away with her hand.

Goodness, she started, where had that thought come from?

"Of course," she parroted stupidly to his reply, hoping that if she kept up a constant stream of babble that he would not get the chance to ask her any more questions. "Why, cricket must be a very popular sport there. What other sports do you engage in, my Lord? Do tell, I'd be most fascinated to hear."

"Sadly, I'm not in the slightest bit fascinated by the thought of listing them off for you," Lord Delaney drawled, his voice laden with sarcasm. "Tell me, Miss Bowstock, are you always this evasive, or is it just with me?"

His direct line of questioning shocked her into silence. Her acting skills were obviously not what she thought them to be, for the Marquess was looking at her with the eyes of a man who knew that she had a secret.

"Other people never give me cause to be evasive," she finally answered, plucking at the skirts of her dress with nervous fingers. "For there are few who would take interest in a Lady's Companion, my Lord. Excepting you, of course."

"So, you admit that you are reluctant to speak of your past?" there was no triumph in his tone and his eyes, when they met Hestia's, were kind.

"If my circumstances had been slightly better, my Lord," Hestia replied, heavily weighting her words so that they were honest and yet revealed little. "Then I would not be a Lady's Companion, I would be someone's wife. A solicitor's maybe, or perhaps a small merchant's."

"I am glad you are nobody's wife."

Goodness, Hestia glanced at the Marquess with utter alarm, was he insinuating that he would like her as his bride? Surely not; perhaps he was going to offer her a position as his mistress, for she knew that wealthy men often did things like that.

"I'm afraid—"

What she was afraid of remained unsaid, for Jane called out for her to play a song on the pianoforte and she readily agreed. Her mother had taught her how to play during the long winters that her father was away at sea and she knew she was as accomplished as any young debutant. Hestia knew all of the proper songs that a young lady ought to know, as well as sadder, more melodic tunes that were native to Cornwall. She was nearing the end of a sweet, poignant song about a sailor lost at sea, when the Marquess came to stand beside her and she lost her place.

"Oh, silly me," she smiled, pushing back her chair without looking at Lord Delaney and going to stand near Jane.

"My dear you have such a sweet voice," the Duchess of Hawkfield cried, "Who taught you how to sing?"

"My mother."

An overwhelming sensation of grief coursed through her and she glanced at Jane, hoping that she might see her distress. Jane, however, was distracted by the ridiculous Mr Jackson, and the only eyes that seemed to witness her grief were those of Lord Delaney, whose sympathetic gaze found hers.

The others were arguing about what activity to play next, with Lady Caroline's suggestion of a board game quickly shot down by her brother.

"How about a game of hide and seek?" Lord Payne asked.

Goodness, Hestia couldn't think of anything worse, but to her surprise the whole group —bar the Duchess, who was going to her chambers— agreed. Giles, Caroline's husband, was chosen as the seeker, and in high-spirits the guests ran from the drawing room, scattering in a dozen different directions.

Hestia, who was not much bothered by winning, scurried toward the library, where she thought she might have a chance to peruse the Duke's book collection while she waited for Giles to find her. The library was situated just off the drawing room, it was a dark, masculine space, lined with mahogany bookshelves that were stuffed with leather bound volumes. She ran an idle finger down the spine of a collection of Lord Byron's works, before plucking it from the shelf and settling down on an over-stuffed Queen Anne by the fireplace. The servants had obviously been busy, as there was a fire dancing happily in the grate, lending the room a cosy air. Imagine having so much wealth that you kept a full fire going in an empty room, just in case you might use it, Hestia thought. There had been one fireplace in the small cottage she had grown up in, and keeping it filled with wood during the winter months had been a constant worry.

Lord Byron's poems were not the most restive of reading materials and after attempting to wade her way through one of his longer sonnets, Hestia stood and padded over to the window. The deep, bay window of the library looked out onto a rose garden, which was in darkness. The sky above was clear with a scattering of stars, that twinkled cheerfully. In Cornwall, the night sky had always seemed endless and magical, stretching to the horizon until it blurred with the sea; but here the sky held no magic for Hestia.

"A penny for your thoughts, Miss Bowstock."

Hestia went rigid with shock at the sound of Falconbridge's voice from behind her. When had he come in? He had either moved in complete silence, or she had been so lost in thought that she had not heard him.

"I don't think they're worth even that," she responded, afraid to turn to look at him. Why was he here? Why could he not just leave her alone, like everybody else? Her status as a servant was supposed to inure her from interest, but it had not deterred the determined Marquess.

"Oh, I don't know," Lord Delaney spoke in a light, teasing tone. "A woman clutching a book of Byron's poems whilst gazing dreamily at the night sky, must surely be thinking something deep and poetic."

"I was thinking of sewing," Hestia responded tartly, offering the dullest topic she could think of. She did not wish to engage in any kind of teasing with Lord Delaney, no matter that his voice left goose pimples on her bare arms.

"Ah, of course you were," he chuckled, a deep, melodic sound that filled the room with warmth. "Were you thinking that the sky is like a beautiful tapestry sewn from glittering silks?"

"No," Hestia replied mulishly, as he came to stand beside her, his arm grazing hers. "I was thinking of my bonnet, which will need a new ribbon sewn onto it."

"Are you always this stubborn?" the Marquess sighed at her answer, looking down at her with eyes that were a mixture of amusement and frustration.

"No," Hestia replied, rather stubbornly, even she had to admit.

"Only with me, then I take it?"

"Well, you insist on following me everywhere," she sighed, her eyes refusing to meet his, "And asking me probing questions that I quite obviously do not wish to answer."

"I am sorry," Falconbridge sounded sincere, his hand reaching for hers, "It was never my intention to make you feel uncomfortable. I am fascinated by you Miss Bowstock and, as an academic, when I am fascinated by a subject, I am filled with a need to know everything that I can possibly know about it."

"There is little to know, my Lord," Hestia's mind was reeling from this startling confession from a man of such a high rank. Her body was responding to his closeness in unfamiliar ways and the feel of his hand holding hers had turned her knees to jelly and her brain to mush. "You know it all, already, my Lord. I fear that I am possibly the dullest creature to have ever walked the earth —I pray, tell me more about you."

"I find it impossible to believe that a woman with such expressive eyes, could ever be dull," Lord Delaney held her gaze. "Though if you would prefer to wait until after we are wed, to reveal yourself completely to me, then so be it."

"Wed?" Hestia balked; goodness this had escalated quickly. "Are you quite well, my Lord? You can't marry me, I am just a servant."

A servant with a criminal father and a history so scandalous that even the Falconbridge's lofty title could not help but be tainted by it.

"Yes, wed," Lord Delaney's eyes danced; he seemed terribly amused by her reaction. "We shall have to for two reasons, the first being that I am attracted to you in a way that I have never felt before."

"And the second?" Hestia asked, wondering if it was she who had gone mad and was hallucinating this absurd conversation.

"Why, because offering for a woman after you have kissed her thoroughly, whilst alone in a dark room, is the honourable thing to do — and I always do the honourable thing. Well, except perhaps for this…"

His lips were upon Hestia's before she had the chance to absorb the intention behind his words. His arms snaked gently around her waist and he pulled her toward him lightly, so that she was pressed against his broad chest. It all happened so quickly and yet, at the same time, it felt as though time had stopped completely. No one had ever kissed her before, nor held her so closely; it was thrilling and terrifying all at once.

"Lud," she whispered in confusion, as he finally broke their spellbinding embrace.

"I'll take that as a compliment," the Marquess's lips quirked in an arrogant smirk. His composure and self-assurance after what, for Hestia, had been a momentous event—her first kiss—irked her.

"It was not a compliment," she whispered waspishly, "You are so arrogant, my Lord. Just because you are a Marquess does not give you the right to kiss me and hold me so closely, when I have given no hint that I wish to be kissed or held."

"You are still in my arms, are you not?"

It was true; Falconbridge's arms were still wrapped around her waist in a possessive manner. Hestia had been enjoying the sensation of being cradled by someone so large and masculine, but she quickly pulled away at his words.

"You took me by surprise," she countered, stepping away from him. She needed to put distance between her body and his, for he radiated a warmth that was overwhelming. "And I think that you must be in your cups, my Lord, to say such strange things and act so rashly."

"I have never been more sober in my life," all teasing had left Falconbridge's voice. "I am immensely attracted to you, I desire you, and I see no reason why we should not be wed."

Hestia could think of one very obvious reason —the Marquess had no idea of her true identity. The second reason, when it struck her, made her realise that she was very much her mother's daughter: he had not said that he loved her.

"Please, I beg you," she said in a voice that was thick with unshed tears. "Do not ask me again, my Lord. It is impossible."

"But why?" Lord Delaney stepped forward, his arms reaching for her again. "Please tell me why it is impossible, Belinda?"

The use of her new moniker was like a slap in the face. Part of her could have been tempted to fall into his arms, to allow him, his title and his wealth to carry her away from her present predicament, but she could not lie to him —no matter how lost and alone she was.

"Because this is not a fairy tale, my Lord," she replied firmly, smoothing down her skirts in an effort to appear calm and collected. "I am not Cinderella, you are not Prince Charming and there will be no happily ever after for us. Now, I beg you, please let me leave."

She would never know if the Marquess would have objected, or put up a fight, against her leaving the room, for outside the door, in the entrance hall, there came the sound of raised voices.

"That sounds like Jane," Hestia cried, gathering her skirts and rushing out of the room. She was greeted by the sight of her mistress, batting away the concern of Giles and Lord Payne, as she made for the staircase.

"Honestly, it's just a migraine," Jane was saying —though Hestia knew from the high-pitch of her voice and its slight tremor, that it was much more than that.

"I will look after Miss Deveraux from here," Hestia said, sweeping out into the hallway and placing herself between Jane and the two men. Jane offered her look of thanks and together the two women climbed the staircase without a backward glance to the men below.

Hestia was most grateful for the distraction of helping Jane to her room, where the misty-eyed young woman confessed that Lord Payne had asked her for her hand —properly this time—and she had said no.

"It's just that I think that Mr Jackson might offer for me," Jane sniffed, "And I have loved him for years. We are both studious, quiet and serious. It would be a much better match."

If Hestia thought that Jane sounded more like she was trying to convince herself, than actually convinced, of Mr Jackson's suitability, she kept her opinion to herself. Jane seemed set on the dull, irritable entomologist and if Hestia said a bad word about him and the pair did marry, then she would soon be out of a job.

The pair parted ways and Hestia undressed for bed. It felt like she had been asleep for only five minutes, when a knocking on the door woke her up. Goodness, she thought as she hurried to open it, was it the Marquess? She would have some very stern words to say to him if it was. She opened the door to find Jane standing outside, her face streaked with tears.

"What on earth?" Hestia exclaimed, worry filling her. She had never seen Miss Deveraux so overwrought; Jane was usually so calm and practical.

"M-M-Mr Jackson thinks me old and unattractive," Jane wailed through her tears.

"Gracious! Did he say that to you?"

"No," Jane's sniffed, her words coming out breathlessly. "I overheard him say it to Lord Payne in the library. Then Lord Payne punched him."

Hestia gave a silent cheer at this news —so she had been right to prefer the heir to Hawkfield over the fusty entomologist.

"I have ruined everything." Jane wailed, a bout of sobbing taking hold again. "I hurt Lord Payne for the sake of Mr Jackson and he has turned out to be an utter cad. Oh, I want to go home to St Jarvis, I don't want to be here anymore."

"It's too late to be running off to Cornwall," Hestia advised, her tone practical. "If you still wish to leave in the morning, then we shall go together. Go to sleep now, Jane. Don't make any rash decisions late at night. Wait until morning, when you feel more rested."

Jane nodded, as though taking her advice and disappeared into her bedchamber, but the next morning when the house woke to find that Jane had disappeared, Hestia knew that her advice had fallen on deaf ears.

8 CHAPTER EIGHT

"Are you quite certain that Jane would have come to Cornwall?" Lord Payne asked Miss Bowstock, for what was probably the millionth time on the journey.

Alex gritted his teeth in annoyance; Belinda had told him a dozen times that Jane was headed for St Jarvis, and yet the heir to Hawkfield insisted on repeating the question. Payne was half convinced that Mr Jackson had kidnapped Miss Deveraux and spirited her away to London, but as her companion had pointed out, a kidnapped woman would not have had the time to pack.

"I'm quite certain," Belinda replied touchily, her eyes focused on the countryside outside the carriage window. Alex refrained from heaving a sigh of annoyance at her resolute determination to look anywhere but at him. When the house had woken to find that Jane had disappeared, Belinda had quickly volunteered to accompany Lord Payne to Cornwall to find her. This had prompted Alex to declare that he too would go, his declaration inspired by the roaring of jealousy within his chest. Lady Caroline had pragmatically said that she would go, so that Miss Bowstock was not travelling across the countryside, alone with two men.

Now, a day later, all four occupants of the carriage were irritable, having spent so long cooped up together, as they raced westward across the English countryside. Determination was a trait that Alex had always thought admirable in a person, but after a day of suffering Belinda determinedly avoiding any eye contact with him, he wasn't so sure.

"We're nearly here," Lord Payne said, with barely concealed relief as the carriage turned onto a coastal road. Alex watched as Belinda leaned forward, her face a picture of excitement.

"Oh, it's beautiful," she whispered, her eyes alight. "I always wanted to visit the North Coast. My father promised he would take me, but he never got a chance before he…"

She stopped speaking abruptly, her face slightly paler than before.

"I did not know your father had died, Miss Bowstock," the Marquess said gently, his first words to her in nearly a day. So Miss Bowstock was an orphan; he had been right, she was truly alone in the world, the realisation made his heartstrings tug in pity for her. "My condolences for your loss."

"Thank you, my Lord," she responded, bestowing upon him a swift, cursory glance, that let Alex know she was not a willing recipient of his pity —or anything else he had to offer her. He scowled; gracious, but she was stubborn.

The carriage trundled past hedgerows filled with early spring flowers; cowslips and daisies danced in long grass, whilst tantalising glimpses of the sea were visible beyond. The conversation in the carriage had dwindled to silence, but as they neared St Jarvis, Lady Caroline began to question her brother on his plan of action.

"I owe Jane a large sum of money for agreeing to pretend to be my betrothed," Lord Payne said with a shrug, ignoring Falconbridge's raised eyebrows, which were in danger of disappearing through the roof of the carriage. So their initial engagement had been a pretence? And Lord Payne had obviously found himself hoist by his own petard and deeply in love with the girl.

"She wanted to buy the boarding house." Pane continued, "If that is still what she wants, then that is what she shall have."

"You're setting her free," Miss Bowstock said, her eyes wide as she marvelled at his words. "Oh, how romantic."

"What utter tosh," Falconbridge was quick to put an end to Belinda's misplaced idea of romanticism. "If you love her, then you must fight for her Payne. Just a few days ago you were ready to put a bullet through Jackson for her hand."

"Jackson's not the obstacle any more, though," James shrugged, in a defeated manner that raised the Marquess's hackles. "It is Jane herself -and you can't suggest I put a bullet through her."

"No," Falconbridge retorted, wondering even as was speaking, if his words were directed to Payne or himself. "Though you can ruddy well tell her that you want her as your wife and that you won't take no for an answer."

He finished this sentence with a pointed look to Miss Bowstock, who flushed and turned her head away quickly. Belinda had been acting as though he had some sort of hideous, contagious disease since the night in the library. He knew that she was not immune to his charms, for he had felt her melt into his embrace and heard the whimpers of longing as he kissed her. What he had proposed was the perfect solution to both their problems; her precarious position as an unwed orphan and his frustration at desperately wanting to possess every part of her…and yet she was resisting. It was altogether most irritating, Alex vowed that once they reached St Jarvis, he would take Miss Bowstock aside and—and… He frowned; there was not much he could do to force Belinda's hand, he could not order her to marry him, no matter what he thought. She was a free agent, she could live her life as she pleased —though he could certainly try to persuade her with more kisses.

He settled back happily into his seat, happy to spend the last few hours of the journey plotting the various ways that he would persuade Miss Bowstock to accept his offer.

The carriage drew up in front of Jarvis House, an impressive pile of bricks, Alex had to admit. Lord Payne leapt from the carriage, without waiting for a footman and barrelled up the steps of the house. Lord Delaney and the two ladies had just disembarked onto the pebbled driveway, when Lord Payne came back out of the house and ran straight past them.

"Where are you going?" Lady Caroline called in frustration after the disappearing figure of her brother.

"The boarding house," Payne cried, sprinting in a manner most unbecoming for a man who would one day be a Duke. Caroline heaved a sigh and glanced apologetically at the Marquess and Miss Bowstock.

"I'm terribly sorry," she said, sounding anything but, "But we shall all have to get back into the carriage —for I'm not about to miss the sight of my brother proposing to his beloved."

And so the trio clambered back inside for the five minute drive to the town of St Jarvis, where the boarding house stood. The door was ajar when they arrived and, with Caroline leading the way, the trio followed the sound of voices to a parlour room, that was stuffed full of women.

Gracious; Falconbridge blinked in surprise, he had never seen so many women gathered together at once, each with their eyes fixed on a flame-cheeked Lord Payne, who was standing beseechingly before Jane.

"What did we miss?" Lady Caroline asked in a stage whisper that echoed across the empty room. Alex tried not to cringe at her obviousness; Payne was in awkward enough a situation without his sister making it worse.

"Lord Payne has told Jane that he loves her and wants her as his bride," a flame-haired woman with a Northern accent deadpanned, "Though he is willing to let her go, if that is what will make her happy."

Alex's attention to the proceedings was distracted somewhat by Miss Bowstock, who had turned a deathly shade of white and begun visibly trembling. As Miss Deveraux and Lord Payne confessed their love for each other, Alex followed the direction of Belinda's gaze to the corner of the room, where an older woman sat. The woman looked rather familiar, though at that moment Lord Delaney could not place her, nor think why her presence had upset Belinda so.

"I will marry you. I will love you for the rest of our days and I will be proud to stand at your side, as your Duchess."

Jane Deveraux's words broke the silence that had fallen in the room and as Lord Payne happily presented his fiancée to all present, a cheer went up. Alex, who had been momentarily distracted by the unfolding drama, spotted that Belinda was discreetly trying to leave the room. He made to follow her, only pausing as the old woman in the corner let out a cry that stopped him mid-step.

"Is that you Hestia?" the woman, who Alex now placed as Mrs Actrol, authoress and sister to Lady Bedford, called.

Miss Bowstock jumped and quite possibly would have fled, if Jane had not borne down on her and embraced her in a warm hug. The wheels and cogs of Alex's brain were whirring away as he watched Jane speak with a nervous looking Belinda.

Hestia, that was what Mrs Actrol had called her. Hestia, the same name as the ward he was searching for, who had mysteriously disappeared. At that very moment he felt something nudging at his boot and looked down to see Henry licking his Hessians with gusto. He could have laughed at his stupidity —when he had visited with Lady Bedford, Mrs Actrol's sister, he had noted that the woman's many Cavaliers had reminded him of Belinda. He realised now that they had reminded him of Belinda because Hestia B. Stockbow and Miss Belinda Bowstock were one and the same.

Fury filled him. How had he been so blinded by the girl's charms that he had failed to see the most obvious clues before him. Bowstock was simply a crude alteration to the name Stockbow—and here he thought he could solve the mysteries of a dead language!

As Lord Payne and Miss Deveraux slipped, unobserved by most, out of the room, the Marquess made his way toward Hestia Stockbow, his mouth a line of grim determination.

"Are you acquainted with Mrs Actrol?" he asked, his tone deliberately light. Those who knew him well, knew that he was at his most dangerous when he acted this calm and controlled, because he was keeping a tight rein on his temper.

"Who?" a pair of big, blue eyes blinked innocently at him, and Alex had to hand it to Miss Stockbow, she did not even glance in Mrs Actrol's direction. Oh, she was very good at this, but he was better and he had the upper hand.

"Really?" he raised an eyebrow, "I thought she called out to you just there. Though she did address you by the wrong name."

"I-I-I don't know what you're talking about, my Lord," Hestia stated, her face pale and her lips trembling. If Alex hadn't been so annoyed at the chit, he would have felt pity toward her.

"I'm sure it was some sort of mix up," he replied, affecting a casual tone, "Come. Allow me to introduce you to Mrs Actrol properly. She's such a fascinating woman and she knows so many different types of people. I'm sure you'll find her most entertaining."

"No," Hestia replied, but Alex had a firm grip on her elbow and he steered her across the crowded drawing room to where the authoress sat. He was surprised that this Hestia Stockbow did not dig her heels into the Oriental rug to halt his progress, such was the look of terror on her face, but she meekly followed him, perhaps accepting that the game was up.

"It is you, Hestia, dear," Mrs Actrol exclaimed happily, as the Marquess deposited Miss Stockbow before her. She peered up at Hestia through her spectacles, her eyes misting with tears.

"My dear, give me a kiss on the cheek. I am mighty pleased to see you looking so well." Mrs Actrol boomed, for she seemed only speak in a voice that was louder than the average. "Despite all the hardships you have endured. I was most sorry to hear about your poor mother —and your father too— Lord rest their souls."

Any feeling of self righteousness that Alex had possessed, fled at the sight of Hestia Stockbow's eyes, which filled with tears at Mrs Actrol's kind words of sympathy. He was a cad, he thought, a complete and utter cad to have subjected the poor girl to this. She was probably petrified, worried that she would lose her position as Jane's companion and end up cast out on the streets.

"And who is this?" Mrs Actrol squinted up at Alex, who drew himself to his full height before bending again in a most perfunctory bow.

"I am Falconbridge, Mrs Actrol," he said, casting Hestia a glance before he spoke again. "I am Miss Stockbow's guardian and future husband."

"You're her what?" Mrs Actrol spluttered, causing several heads to turn their way.

"I am the legal guardian of Miss Hestia B. Stockbow, as appointed by her father David Stockbow in his last will and testament," Falconbridge repeated slowly. "And, besides that, Miss Stockbow and I are to be wed. As soon as I return her to London and procure the necessary paperwork of course."

"Oh, of course," Mrs Actrol echoed him before breaking down into gales of laughter that wracked her generous frame. "Though, my Lord, you seem to have lost your ward.."

What? Alex looked to his right, where a second ago Hestia had been standing and found that she had disappeared; he scanned the room and spotted her closing the door to the hallway behind her as she fled.

"You'll have to keep a closer eye on that one, my Lord, if you're intent on making her your bride," Mrs Actrol offered her advice with a knowing smile. "For she's the daughter of a man who escaped capture for decades

—don't think she didn't pick a trick or two up from old David."

The sound of the authoress' laughter followed Alex as he made his way out of the room, the fury he had been working so hard to control threatening to bubble over and cause a catastrophe.

9 CHAPTER NINE

She needed to escape.

Hestia's heart pounded in her chest as she pushed her way through the drawing room, past so many unfamiliar faces and out into the hallway. She closed the door behind her firmly, wondering how best to extricate herself from the unbelievable situation that had suddenly been thrust upon her.

Lord Delaney was her guardian?

The idea was so absurd, that if she had not been in such a panic, she would have laughed. How had her father thought to appoint the Marquess of Falconbridge as her legal guardian? She could think of no connection that would tie the perfect and respectable Lord Delaney to her criminal father —except...

Her mother.

A conversation that Hestia had heard, all those years ago, came back to her. Her mother's cousin Amelia had married a Marquess; it must have been Falconbridge.

Oh, this was terrible, for it meant that the already overbearing, self-entitled Lord had every right to act in his usual bossy manner around her —even more so, as he was her guardian. He would be even more insufferable than usual, now he had this to leverage over her. Hestia scurried up the hallway, determined to flee the boarding house and the village of St Jarvis at once.

She would never solve the mystery of what had happened to her father if Lord Delaney thought he was in charge of her. He would lock her up in some God forsaken estate, for her own safety and protection, and leave her there until she was a dusty old maid. Hestia quickened her pace and would have made it to freedom, had her way not been blocked by Jane and Lord Payne, who were engaged in an amorous embrace.

"Oh, Belinda, it's you!" Jane broke away from her betrothed at the sound of Hestia's footsteps, her face beet-red with embarrassment. Lord Payne, on the other hand, did not look in the least bit bashful at having been caught out kissing his future bride, instead he looked pleased as punch.

"I need to go—I need to go—" Hestia stuttered, wishing she could just shove the pair out of her way.

"Oh-ho!" Lord Payne nodded in understanding, "I think you'll find it's upstairs somewhere."

"I beg your pardon?" Hestia, who had been distracted by the sound of the drawing room door opening, turned to look at Lord Payne in confusion. Realisation dawned on her, after a moment, and her face flamed as red as Jane's. "No. Not that, my Lord. I need to go outside. Now. Please excuse me."

The lovestruck pair stood back, to allow Hestia pass, their faces wearing identical expressions of confusion.

"But where are you going, Belinda?" Jane asked, her brow creased in a frown; she was unused to the meek and timid Belinda Bowstock acting in such a firm manner. But she was not Belinda Bowstock, Hestia thought grimly, she was Hestia B. Stockbow and she needed to flee.

"She is going nowhere."

It was too late, she thought, as she turned to find the towering form of the Marquess behind her —though it had always been too late, for her plan had been silly, born out of panic. There was no way that she would have out-run Lord Delaney with a mere three second head start. Observing his dark, angry face, Hestia thought that she'd need a three week head start if she was actually to stand a chance.

"Good heavens, my Lord," Jane, who was usually a most mild mannered individual, rounded on the Marquess, wagging her finger as she spoke. "I will not have you terrify my companion again. You've already done it once and now you seek to do it once more—with witnesses, no less! Whatever has come over you? You usually have impeccable manners."

"What has come over me?" Lord Delaney questioned mildly, his eyes on Hestia. "Do you know, Miss Deveraux, I'm not certain that I could explain it properly myself. Why don't you ask Miss Hestia Stockbow here to fill you in on a few details you might be missing?"

"Who on earth is Hestia Stockbow?" Jane looked from Hestia to the Marquess, and back again, in confusion.

"I am."

Never before had Hestia silenced a room, but there was always a first for everything, she thought wryly as her quiet confession rendered her mistress and Lord Payne mute.

"Stockbow, Stockbow…Why does that name sound so familiar?" Jane pondered aloud, after an eternity of silence.

"My father was in the papers of late," Hestia mumbled, her cheeks burning red. "David Stockbow…"

"Oh, the pirate!" Lord Payne exclaimed, his face lighting up with excitement. "Why, you never said Belinda, I mean Hestia. I mean. Lud, I don't know what I mean."

"I was afraid that I would not find a position unless I lied about my family name," Hestia ignored Lord Payne's confused outburst and turned, instead to Jane. "I am sorry that I misled you Jane, and I beg your forgiveness."

"Pshaw,"Jane waved an airy hand, her eyes dancing with excitement. "Of course you had to lie, my dear. Emily's mother would never have accepted you for the position if there had been any hint of a scandal attached to you. Oh, Hestia, you should have told me! I have so many questions, piracy is a most fascinating topic. Did you know that the earliest documented instance of pirates attacking, was in the 14th century, when the so-called Sea Peoples attacked the ships of the Aegean and Mediterranean civilisations?"

"No,I did not know that" Hestia bit her lip to keep the giggles that were threatening at bay. Did Miss Deveraux honestly think that her father's murky past was an opportunity for an impromptu history lesson?

"Oh, but piracy has a most fascinating history that stretches back even further than this century," Jane continued, buoyed by her favourite topic of conversation, "Ancient Greeks actually condoned piracy as a viable profession; it apparently was widespread and regarded as an perfectly honourable way of making a living."

"Is that so?" Hestia asked, her eyebrows raised in what she hoped was an expression of interest, rather than the bemusement she actually felt.

"Oh, yes. I know when I was studying—"

"Excuse me," the Marquess finally found his voice, interrupting Jane mid-speech. "We are not here for a lecture on the history of pirates. We are here to discuss Miss Hestia Stockbow; your companion and my ward."

"Your ward?"

Judging by the expression of horror on Jane's face, she found the idea that Hestia was the Marquess's ward far more shocking than the fact that her companion's father had once been a thief of the high seas. If the situation hadn't been so serious, Hestia would have laughed, for Jane was full of surprises.

"Yes. My ward," the Marquess cast Hestia a possessive glance, "And once we return to London, she will be my bride."

"Hold up, old fellow. Did I miss something?" Lord Payne asked in bemusement, "I thought I just heard you say that you intend to marry Miss Bowstock —I mean Stockbow."

"I do," the Marquess spoke in a pompous manner, drawing himself up to his full height as he did so. "For two reasons, the first being that she needs the protection of my name, the second being that I compromised her honour."

"You did not compromise my honour," Hestia interjected testily —who did he think he was, announcing that to her employer? All they had shared was a brief kiss, and no one would ever have known of it, if he hadn't blabbered so.

"Yes, I did," Lord Delaney smiled at her in a most patronising manner. "That night in the Library in Hawkfield Manor."

"That was just a kiss," Hestia snapped, his self satisfied smile filling her with rage. "A mere peck, stolen I might add, by you."

She watched in satisfaction as the Marquess turned a rather alarming shade of red at her dismissive remark. It gave her a slight thrill to know that she could fluster him in the same way that he had left her flustered in the library.

"Nevertheless, your honour was compromised, and we must wed," Falconbridge stated, through gritted teeth, obviously deciding to ignore her.

"My honour was not compromised, though if you insist on shouting that it was people will start to believe you."

Hestia and the Marquess were squared off in the centre of the hallway, almost nose to nose, and they would surely have begun a most undignified shouting match, had Lord Payne not spoken.

"How would that work out then, Falconbridge, I wonder?" he asked casually, a grin threatening to erupt across his handsome face. "You being Miss Stockbow's guardian, would mean that to defend her honour, you'd have to call the man who allegedly besmirched it out. Though you can't very well call yourself out, now can you?"

"No, I can't."

Hestia thought that the Marquess's head might explode, or at the very least steam might start pouring out his ears, as he digested Lord Payne's silly observation. The laughter that had been threatening finally bubbled over and she found herself wiping tears of mirth away.

"She's hysterical with nerves," Falconbridge muttered, glancing at Hestia in alarm. Even Jane looked rather worried as she took in the sight of her companion, bent double, as laughter wracked her frame.

"I shall have to send for a physician," Falconbridge continued, running an agitated hand through his thick hair. "She'll need some smelling salts —or perhaps a tonic of some sort."

"What I need," Hestia, who had finally stopped laughing said, "Is a cup of tea and a rational discussion on what I am supposed to do, now that the secret of my identity has been revealed."

She would never know what the Marquess's response to her demands would have been, for a cheerful Northern voice spoke, startling them all.

"I don't know much about secret identities," a flame haired woman said cheerfully, as she came bustling down the hallway. "But I do know a lot about tea, and I know that Mrs Actrol has asked that I serve my best brew in the parlour for her old friend Hestia —and anyone who has an interest in

Hestia's wellbeing."

Hestia watched, overwhelmed with gratitude, as Jane gave a firm nod and said; "That would be me."

"And me," the Marquess added.

Fiddlesticks.

It was rather a surreal experience, watching three people discuss her future as though she were not there. Mrs Actrol, Jane and the Marquess of Falconbridge had been going back and forth for the past half hour, arguing amongst themselves on the best course of action for Hestia's future.

Jane was adamant that Hestia stay with her, while the Marquess kept making dark noises about London and special licences, that Jane did her best to ignore.

The debate was chaired by Mrs Actrol, who would interject occasionally, to question the two on minor details that they had overlooked.

"Stockbow made you the executioner of his will, Falconbridge," the older woman stated, her blue eyes thoughtful behind her spectacles, "Did he leave Hestia anything of worth?"

"Just the cottage near Truro," Falconbridge shrugged dismissively, "Which would be better off condemned, than lived in. He left no money, just several small debts, which have been looked after."

Hestia flushed at this, who had looked after them? She glanced sideways at the Marquess, whose face was impassive, and knew instinctively that it had been him. Oh, she was already in his debt and she had no way of paying him back.

"Could you live there happily, Hestia?" Mrs Actrol questioned gently. "It has been your home for all your life, after all."

Hestia thought of the tumbledown cottage, where both her father and mother's lives had ended so sadly. She thought of the village, where she had few friends, and would have even fewer now because of the scandal, and shook her head.

"I think I would be best to stay in a large town or city," she decided firmly, "Your sister was right, Mrs Actrol, when she said that there was no future for me there."

She did not want to say it aloud, especially in front of the Marquess, but Hestia knew that one day she wanted to marry and have children, and nobody would offer for her with such a chequered family history.

"I don't know why we're even discussing this," the Marquess drawled in annoyance. His dark gaze caught Hestia's, leaving her slightly breathless at its intensity. "Miss Stockbow is my ward, as her legal guardian any decisions to be made on her future will be made by me."

"While dictating to the girl sounds nice in theory, my Lord," Mrs Actrol responded in a mildly amused tone. "It will not work in practice. Did you not see her bolt from the room today? She very nearly got away from you. Given an undesirable situation and time to formulate a plan, Hestia will disappear altogether."

The Marquess made a sound that was halfway between a grunt and a cough, clearly annoyed by the older woman's rationale. For a moment Hestia felt a thrill of victory, until the authoress looked at her sternly over her spectacles.

"That's not to say that I don't think what the Marquess is offering you is your best option, Hestia," she said grimly. "Your situation is most dire. The protection of his name would grant you leave to live a full life, which you otherwise may never be able to do. Stability, comfort, a title; these are not things to turn your nose up at, my dear."

"What about love?" Jane spoke quietly, turning her blushing face to Lord Payne as she spoke. Hestia flinched at the mention of that word; love had led her parents to an early grave, she wanted nothing to do with it.

"Love is a luxury," Mrs Actrol shrugged, "Respect and mutual understanding quite often act as the best foundations for a marriage."

"It's lucky I don't lack for confidence," the Marquess snorted, as the group descended into a thoughtful silence. "Any other man would find having the drawbacks and benefits of his marriage proposal discussed so openly rather demoralising."

"Luckily you're not any other man," Mrs Actrol answered tartly, her eyes sparkling with amusement. Hestia knew the woman well enough to know that she was rather enjoying taking the stuffy Marquess down a peg or two. "And you can understand why a girl like Hestia might be doubtful about placing her future in the hands of a man so senior."

"I am but four and thirty," the Marquess blustered with indignation, small patches of red staining his cheeks. "I hardly have one foot in the grave. Now —if you are all done, I would like to have a word alone with Miss Stockbow."

When no one made a move to leave, Falconbridge cast an icy glare around the room.

"Either you all leave, or I carry Miss Stockbow off to London this second."

"If you need me, I'll be just outside," Jane whispered as she passed Hestia. The trio traipsed out of the parlour, leaving Hestia alone with the Marquess. Once the door had closed behind their companions, Falconbridge stood and began to pace the small room. He was so tall, she marvelled as she watched him pace to and fro upon the chintz rug; well over six foot by her estimation. Falconbridge stopped pacing abruptly, turned and ran an agitated hand through his hair.

"Honour dictates that I propose to you," he stated baldly. "It was my intention to marry you before I knew of your true identity. Learning that your safety has been entrusted to me only doubles that determination."

"I would not want you to think of me as a burden," Hestia retorted, "Or an obligation to be fulfilled."

"You are neither, I promise you that." All the acrimony had left him and he watched her with kind, sincere eyes. It would be so easy to fall in love with a man like the Marquess, Hestia thought sadly, a noble man who wanted to always do the honourable thing.

"I shall not press you, for anything that you do not wish to give, until you are ready," he added lightly. It took Hestia a moment to fully understand the weight of his words, and once she did, she felt her cheeks flame. She had not even thought of that aspect of marriage, and here he was mentioning it as casually as though he were remarking upon the weather.

"You are a clever girl, Miss Stockbow, surely you must understand that marriage is the best course of action?"

"My father was murdered," was what she finally decided upon as her response. "If we wed, my Lord, will you help me find out who did it?"

"I promise."

If the Marquess thought her request strange, his face did not betray him; instead he looked at her with thinly veiled apprehension, as though he still thought she would bolt.

"Shall I take it that you consent?" he finally asked.

"I do," Hestia whispered, already wondering if she had made a grave mistake.

10 CHAPTER TEN

If Alex had forgotten how much he despised society, he was soon reminded of it a week later. It was a warm Thursday evening in St James' Square. An earlier bout of spring rain had cleared the usually smoky London sky, so that from the window of the carriage, Alex was able to see a spectacular sun setting over the rooftops.

His gaze was aimed upward, in appreciation of the heavenly sky, as if he looked out at ground level, he would most surely scream.

Traffic.

Dozens of carriages were snaking their way around the square, at a speed slower than a funeral procession, all headed in the same direction: the Duke of Hawkfield's residence. Not for the first time, Alex turned to his sister and grumbled; "It would be far quicker if we just got out and walked."

"Don't be silly, dear," Phoebe, Lady Thackery sighed. "Nobody arrives on foot to a ball, it's not the done thing."

Alex was about to retort that he did not give a fig for the "done thing", when he caught sight of Hestia's pale face. She was seated beside Phoebe, wearing an expression that one might expect to see on a man condemned to death and not a young girl on the way to her first ball. Having a great antipathy toward balls in general, Alex emphasised with her feelings, though he knew that Hestia's fears ran deeper than his own misgivings, which were purely down to his own impatience with the feckless members of the ton.

Tonight was the night that Hestia Stockbow was to meet London Society, no wonder the poor girl looked pained, for her arrival in London had been talked about by all and sunder —even warranting a column or two in the papers.

After seeing all the furore over her arrival in town, it had been decided by his sister and Miss Deveraux, that the best way to introduce Hestia to the *beau monde*, was as the close friend of some of society's most powerful people. The Duke and Duchess of Hawkfield, as well as the Duke and Duchess of Everleigh had been rallied to the cause, each couple promising to let it be known of their fondness for Miss Stockbow.

Phoebe, who was herself married to an Earl, had taken Hestia under her wing in a way that Alex could not dare have hoped for. Hestia had been deposited at Lord and Lady Thackery's home a week ago, after a long trip from Cornwall, to live under Phoebe's care until the necessary paper-work was in place for the wedding. Alex had been loathe to part with his intended just for proprieties' sake, though his rather bossy older-sister had shot down his declaration that he too would stay at Thackery Hall until the wedding.

"For heaven's sake Alex," Phoebe had admonished, "Use that brain of yours, the one that everyone is always harping on about. Miss Stockbow has enough black marks against her name, without the rumour that you are living together in sin circulating. Besides, the sight of your grumpy face in the morning would put me off my breakfast."

"Don't fear, Miss Stockbow," Alex had said, ignoring his sister's barbs, instead addressing Hestia; "You shan't be left here for long."

"Actually, I think I'll rather enjoy my stay with your sister," Hestia had responded, evidently delighted to see someone speak down to him. At the time, Alex had rather regretted leaving Hestia under Phoebe's bad influence, but having seen her tonight, he had to concede that his sister had done a marvellous job with the young lady who would be his bride.

Gone was the hideous bonnet and the dowdy dresses, replaced instead by an elegant chignon and a dress of sapphire blue, that clung to her every curve. For the first time in his life he wished that he knew more about women's fashion, so that he could commission a modiste to make a hundred dresses for Hestia, all in that same soft, puffy material.

She was like a cloud come to earth for one night, he decided, not caring that this was a ridiculously sappy thing for a man who had been to war to think.

The carriage trundled on, eventually arriving at the front steps of Hawkfield House, the imposing, three-story residence of the Duke and Duchess.

"It would have taken us five minutes by foot," Alex grumbled again to his sister, as a footman opened the door, for his own home was just around the corner on the equally affluent Duke Street.

Phoebe ignored him, instead tucking Hestia's arm under her own as she marched up the steps to the front door. Alex followed, reluctantly deciding that he had done enough grumbling for one night. Tonight was about Hestia, about making sure that she had the smoothest possible entry to society as was possible. It was not an opportunity for him to display his famous impatience.

The ballroom of Hawkfield House was packed to bursting, which was an impressive feat, as it was one of the largest ballrooms in all of England. A slight hush fell over the crowd, as their arrival was announced, and Alex saw several people craning to get a better look at Hestia. His protective instincts kicked in, and he was filled with a need to shield her from view.

Don't be ridiculous, he chastised himself, there's no point in taking her out, just to hide her away. Indeed, Hestia appeared to be handling the attention rather well. She walked a little before him, her shoulders back and her head held high. As they made their way past the crowds, Alex heard a few people exclaiming how pretty Miss Stockbow was.

"I suppose it's true that men lose all their senses at the sight of a pretty face," a nasally voice whispered loudly as they passed, "For Falconbridge must have near lost his mind, if he intends to sully the line by marrying the girl."

Alex whipped around, to see who had spoken, but all he saw were curious faces staring back at him. He hoped that Hestia had not heard, though judging by the stiffness of her shoulders, she had.

"There you are Hestia, dearest."

It was Jane, dressed in a dove grey gown, which complimented her creamy complexion and rosy cheeks. The future Duchess of Hawkfield bestowed two kisses on Hestia's cheeks and drew her towards her conspiratorially.

"Everyone is so glad you could make it. Come, my Lord, my Lady, Lord Payne's parents and the Duke and Duchess of Everleigh are awaiting your arrival."

Alex followed a step behind as Hestia was led toward the two Dukes and Duchesses. There were few among the ton who could claim an association with either family, to be so publicly welcomed by both was quite the *coup d'état*. Olive, Duchess of Ashford smiled warmly as Hestia was presented to her.

"How wonderful to meet you again, Miss Stockbow," she said loudly, so that the shameless earwigs standing nearby would overhear. "I am so looking forward to renewing our acquaintance, now you are back in town."

"And I yours, your Grace," Hestia mumbled, her cheeks pink.

The Duke and Duchess of Hawkfield were no less gracious and, once the introductions were finished, instructed Hestia and Alex to enjoy the festivities.

"I cannot allow Miss Stockbow leave, until she promises me a dance," the Duke of Everleigh called. "I am certain she will be much in demand for the night."

"Yes," even though he knew that Everleigh was only trying to show kindness, Alex felt himself bristle with indignation; "She will be busy dancing with me."

"Though of course, when my brother can be persuaded to leave Hestia's side, she will be delighted to dance with you, your Grace," Phoebe interjected swiftly, with a sharp elbow to Alex's ribs to silence him.

He glowered, but kept his peace, for he knew that Phoebe was right to chastise him for his ill manners. He could not expect Hestia to have a successful launch into society if he did not allow her to speak to anyone bar him. After the wedding, he thought, they would have all the time in the world together. Perhaps he would take her away, down to the small estate he owned near Penzance, and they could spend some time alone together, away from prying eyes.

His sister stole Hestia away soon after, leaving Alex to moodily stalk the periphery of the ballroom. He nodded at the many familiar faces he passed, though engaged none in conversation. A familiar fop of blonde hair, however, drew him from his reclusive state.

"Pierre," he called, clapping his fellow academic heartily on the back, "This was the last place I was expecting to find you."

"It is the last place I expected to be," the Frenchman replied with a weak smile, "However the Duke kindly invited me last week, when he paid a visit to Montagu House to check on *our* progress."

Alex could not help but note the tone of disapproval in Dubois' voice as he spoke of their shared project. Since meeting Miss Stockbow, Alex had been rather neglecting his work on translating the Egyptian steele, and it was clear that the French man was annoyed.

"I know I have not been very helpful," he offered an apology with a rueful grin, "But I inherited a ward, then found myself a bride and all thought of translation simply left my head. Once the wedding is over and done with, I'll be back to my old self."

"Yes," Dubois lowered his voice to a whisper, so low that Alex had to lean in to hear him. "Do you think she knows where the missing piece of the stone is, this Stockbow girl? Is that why you're marrying her?"

His question shocked Alex for two reasons; the first being that he had forgotten Dubois knew of David Stockbow's connection to the missing stone, the second being that he himself had been so overcome by feelings for Hestia that her connection to the missing piece of stone, hadn't even registered.

"I have not yet asked her," he replied truthfully, which made Dubois sigh with irritation.

"For goodness sake, just ask the girl. She must know where it is! What's the point of having her as your wife, if she doesn't lead you to the stone?"

Alex felt slightly uncomfortable at Dubois's insinuation that he was only marrying Hestia in the hope that she might reveal where —or if—her father had hidden the steele. Dubois's words perfectly showed his focused determination to decipher the mysteries of Egyptian hieroglyphics, at any cost. In fact, Alex was certain, if Dubois had stumbled upon Hestia before he had, that the Frenchman would have married her instead of him.

"Must dash, old fellow, my sister is beckoning for me," Alex offered apologetically, hoping that Dubois would not look over his shoulder and find that Phoebe was doing no such thing. Alex pushed his way through the throngs of people, to where his sister and his intended stood, deep in conversation Lady Caroline, Lord Payne's sister.

"There you are," Phoebe called brightly, as he arrived at her side. "You're just in time for the first dance of the night."

Indeed, the orchestra, who had been warming up, struck up the first notes of a Quadrille just as Phoebe finished her sentence. Alex would rather have shared a more intimate waltz with Miss Stockbow, but he chivalrously took her hand and led her out onto the floor.

"I have never danced in public, my Lord," she whispered, her petrified eyes darting to and fro, as though plotting an escape route.

"But you know the steps?" Alex questioned.

She nodded and he gave her an encouraging smile; "That's all that is required, I swear. Everyone will be too wrapped up in themselves to pay you any heed."

This was, in fact, a bare-faced lie; Alex knew full well that the whole room was watching as he and Hestia joined three other couples, for the set dance, though he wasn't about to share that with her. The dance was a lively number, and soon Hestia's face was pink with exertion and excitement. As the music came to an end, Hestia's hand was holding Alex's and he silently marvelled at how perfectly they fit together.

He led her from the ballroom floor, heading through the crowd toward his sister, who was chatting animatedly with friends by the bowls of ratafia. Alex had a sneaking suspicion that her animation was partly fuelled by the sweet alcohol, for she seemed even more exuberant than usual.

Hestia, who had appeared relaxed after their energetic dance, suddenly stiffened beside him. Alex glanced at her with concern, following her frightened gaze to where a tall man of about forty, with a shock of floppy, blonde hair stood.

Lord Bleakly, Viscount Havisham —Alex recognised him from White's, though he had not thought of the familial connection that the Viscount shared with his betrothed.

The whole room seemed to have noticed Hestia's discomfort and were watching gleefully, to see what would unfold. Would the Viscount snub his niece? It would be the talk of the town for weeks, if he did.

Havisham paled, as he sighted his niece. Alex witnessed a multitude of emotions flicker across the Viscount's face, until he finally settled on a look of resignation. He said a quiet word to the gentleman he had been conversing with and ambled over to the Marquess and Hestia.

"Delaney," he called, in a voice slightly louder than was usual, which Alex assumed was for the benefit of the listening crowd. "My congratulations. I wish you and my niece every happiness for your shared future together."

As the two men briefly clasped hands in an awkward handshake, Alex swore he could almost feel a rush of air, as the crowd sighed with disappointment: there would be no scandal to discuss the next morning. That Lord Bleakly did not actually talk to his niece, nor even glance at her, and instead directed his words at the Marquess, was neither here nor there. As the night drew to a close, Alex happily decided that Hestia's launch had been a resounding success, and that things could only get easier from here on in.

11 CHAPTER ELEVEN

In the past fortnight Hestia's life had changed so much, that sometimes she found herself pinching her arm, to ensure that she wasn't simply dreaming.
She had gone from the position of lowly paid companion, to the honoured guest of an Earl and Countess, and with that had come a plethora of luxuries. Her bedroom was no longer a small, cramped servant's room on the top floor of the house, but an enormous suite of rooms on the first floor, complete with four poster bed and a feather mattress. The bed chamber alone was nearly the size of the entire cottage that she had grown up in and she found its proportions a little overwhelming.
Henry, who had always had delusions of grandeur, had settled in rather well to his new accommodation, though Hestia still felt a little nervous at her grand surroundings, she had, however, grown very fond of her hostess.
Phoebe, Lady Thackery was quite different to her brother. Where the Marquess was cool and aloof, his sister was warm and open. She treated Hestia like an equal, taking her with her on her morning calls, and accompanying her to a *modiste*, who was commissioned to make the future Marchioness of Falconbridge a dozen new dresses.
"I can't allow you to spend so much money, my Lady," Hestia had stuttered, red-faced at the extravagance.
"Oh, don't be silly dear. It's not my money, it's Alex's," Lady Thackery had responded happily. "He has given me *carte blanche* to spend what I like on your new wardrobe. And how many times must I tell you, call me Phoebe."
Once Hestia's wardrobe was filled with six day dresses, a riding habit and several beautiful ball-gowns, a notice was put in the paper to find her a lady's maid. If somebody had told Hestia a year ago, that she would need someone to help her dress every morning, she would have said they were fit for Bedlam. Having witnessed the complicated strings, bows and laces attached to her stays and new dresses, Hestia soon relented that lady's maid was, in fact, a necessity for a lady.
The girl who was hired, Catherine, had auburn hair and an unplacable accent.

"My last mistress was married to an Irish Earl and I spent many years there, near Kerry," was all she offered, when Hestia questioned it one morning. Although the girl was reticent to offer details of her past employment, she was in general, good company for Hestia, who enjoyed listening to her melodic, lilting voice.

Catherine accompanied her everywhere, and when she wasn't shadowed by her lady's maid, she was with Lady Thackery and frequently the Marquess, who called every day. That she and Lord Delaney were to be wed, still seemed like a faintly ridiculous notion to Hestia. Sometimes she was so overwhelmed at the idea of becoming his wife, that she felt she could bolt, but there was always someone present to prevent her escape.

I just need a morning to myself, to think, she thought with despair after another round of house-calls with Lady Thackery. As it happened once they arrived home, Phoebe, who was usually brimming with energy, declared herself exhausted and repaired to her rooms for a nap. Catherine, who had joined Henry as Hestia's second shadow, looked at Hestia expectantly, waiting to be told what to do next.

"Would you like to take the afternoon off, Catherine?" Hestia asked, trying to keep the hopeful note from her voice. "We've been so busy these past few days, I'm sure you are as exhausted as I."

"I can help you get ready for bed, ma'am," Catherine offered.

"Oh, thank you, but no," Hestia replied firmly, "I think I'll just stay in my room and read. Off you go, put your feet up. I'll call if I need you."

Hestia waited until she was certain that the girl had gone up to her room, before grabbing Henry's leash from her bedroom, and slipping out the servant's door at the rear of the house.

Freedom.

She pulled her shawl tightly around her, to ward off the brisk Spring air, and hurried down Dover Street, toward Piccadilly. The footpaths were crowded with people from all walks of life, and too late Hestia thought of the hem of her dress, which was soon spattered with mud. Ladies did not walk places for a reason, she thought, as she surveyed her dress with dismay.

At Piccadilly she crossed the road, weaving through carriages and carts, until she reached the far footpath and the entrance to Green Park. At last, she thought happily, slowing her pace as she began her stroll through the lush, green park-lands.

Henry, who had been reluctant to leave the comfort of Thackery House, perked up at the familiar surroundings of Green Park. Hestia untied his leash and watched with satisfaction as he tore off across the fields, his tail wagging with excitement.

If only life could always be like this, she thought, as she followed the path farther into the park, where it was less crowded. She did like London, she liked the hustle and bustle that came with living in a large city, but at heart she was just a country mouse. She was also just a plain, un-titled, young woman; unused to the demands of society. Every day for the past fortnight, she had been paraded before the madams of the ton and her cheeks ached from smiling politely, while her head ached from trying to remember the strict social protocols she was supposed to adhere to.

It was all too much, she thought, and it was all distracting her from the pressing matter of finding out who it was that had murdered her father. Lord Delaney, who had danced attendance on her since their betrothal, had failed to mention the promise he had made to help her discover what had happened that fateful night in Cornwall. Any time she tried to raise the subject with him, he changed topic quickly, instead preferring to talk about their upcoming nuptials.

She was so frustrated that she could scream, and she knew that if she screamed, her ire would be directed at the Marquess, who kept insisting she call him Alex.

"Oh, Henry," she whispered to her small canine companion, who had returned from his explorations. "What am I to do?"

If Henry had any wisdom to offer, he kept his silence, though he did nudge her hand with his cool, wet nose, demanding a pat. Hestia happily obliged him before continuing with her stroll. She had been walking for about half an hour, when she crossed paths with a blonde haired man, who did a double take when he saw her approaching.

"Miss Stockbow," the man called, in accented English. "How 'appy I am to make your acquaintance."

"I am sorry, Sir, I do not know your name."

Hestia's thoughts instantly flew to the Marquess, and his words of warning that Green Park was not a safe place for a lady to walk alone. The man opposite her looked safe enough, he wore an elegant dark coat over breeches and boots, which looked as expensive as anything Falconbridge might wear.

"Ah, of course, My apologies - I am Pierre Dubois. I am sure that Lord Delaney has told you all about me."

"Ah," Hestia wracked her brain trying to remember if the Marquess had ever mentioned the French man to her.

"I see he has not mentioned me at all," Dubois huffed, a flash of annoyance crossing his long, thin face. "I am not surprised; he seems to have completely forgotten me and our work, since meeting you."

"I am sorry," Hestia offered, wondering why she was apologising, when it was the Marquess who was at fault. "Do you study hieroglyphics as well?"

"I do not study them," Dubois replied arrogantly, "I live and breathe them. Tell me, has Lord Delaney mentioned the missing stone to you?"

"No," Hestia answered honestly, she hadn't the faintest idea what the

Frenchman was speaking of. He narrowed his eyes in annoyance at her reply and heaved an irritated sigh.

"For the past year, Falconbridge and I have been trying to decipher a steele from ancient Egypt. Our progress is being hampered by the fact that a large piece of it is missing. The missing piece was thought to have been stolen by pirates, who attacked a British Navy ship. The man suspected of this act of theft was none other than your father."

Dubois finished speaking and looked at her pointedly, waiting for her response, but Hestia was speechless at his revelation.

"Has Lord Delaney not yet asked you if you know where the stone might be?" he questioned impatiently.

When Hestia shook her head, he clucked his tongue in disapproval.

"Honestly, there is no point in pussyfooting around the question. *Do* you know where it might be? Did your father ever tell you where he hid his treasures?"

"My father pawned nearly everything he stole," she whispered, delivering her words in a voice that shook with threatened tears. "He wasn't particularly adept at managing his finances. If he had stolen that stone that you are looking for, Sir, then I regret to inform you that it could be anywhere. Perhaps try Mr Meagher's Pawn Shop, in Truro. He might remember purchasing it from my father."

"Truro," Dubois gave a snort, "I'm not trekking all the way back there again."

"Again?" Hestia tried to keep her voice steady as she spoke, ignoring her heart which was hammering a wild tattoo in her chest.

"I was there a few months ago," Dubois gave a Gallic shrug, "Hoping that I might find some information on the stone. My journey bore little fruit, sadly. When Falconbridge said he was marrying you, I hoped that you might be useful to our search. I can see I was wrong. Good day, Miss Stockbow."

Pierre Dubois touched the brim of his hat in a goodbye salutation, leaving Hestia standing alone on the path, rooted to the spot in shock.

Her mind was whirring as she tried to register all that had transpired. This man, this blonde man, had been in Truro just before her father's death. He obviously believed that David Stockbow had stolen the stone, and he certainly seemed obsessed by getting it back.

Was it possible that Pierre Dubois had killed her father?

A chill wind brought her mind back to the present and she decided that she had had enough of Green Park. Hestia hurried back the path she had come down, clutching her shawl tightly around her body for warmth. There was something else bothering her, something that Dubois had said.

He had questioned if Falconbridge had asked her "yet" where the stone might be, which implied that the two men had been discussing her. It also implied that the Marquess, for all his talk of honour, chivalry and responsibility, had ulterior motives when he had asked her to be his bride. Anger began to simmer within and by the time that Hestia arrived back at the Thackery's Mayfair home, her fury was fit to boil over.

"Where on earth have you been?"

The authoritative tone of the Marquess as he greeted her in the entrance hall, did little to dampen Hestia's rage. His handsome face wore a look of smug superiority, and he seemed filled with righteous indignation. Well, she'd show him indignation.

"Out for a walk," she snapped, as she passed her shawl to a waiting footman, who quickly disappeared with it.

"Alone?"

If she had not been so angry herself, the icy fury in that one word would have petrified her. Falconbridge's expression was thunderous at her revelation that she had walked alone, despite his previously having forbid it.

"No. Not alone, I brought Henry," Hestia said, tugging at the buttons of her gloves as she struggled to take them off. "And I met your friend Mr. Dubois. Tell me, my Lord, when were you going to reveal to me that you thought I was keeping the location of stolen historical artifacts a secret? Before or after the wedding?"

His stunned silence was most gratifying. Hestia checked a victorious smile that was threatening and concentrated instead on trying to unbutton her gloves, which was proving a most difficult task.

"Here," the Marquess finally said, coming to stand beside her, "Allow me."

He took her hand in his and began to undo the dozen or so buttons which ran from her elbow to her wrist. He worked quickly to free one hand, but took his time over the second glove. She watched, a little breathlessly, as he worked his way, painstakingly slowly, to the final button. She had not known that such a simple act could be turned into something that felt almost sinfully intimate.

"Please believe me," Falconbridge said, as he pulled the glove from her hand. "That your father's connection to my work, in no way influenced my decision to marry you. In fact, until Dubois mentioned it, it had completely left my mind."

"Why should I believe you?" Hestia questioned.

"Because I am telling the truth."

Falconbridge took her bare hand in his and squeezed it tightly, before holding it against his broad chest. Hestia could feel his heart thumping within, and was startled to find that its beat was as erratic as her own; was it possible that the Marquess had been as affected by their interaction as she? It was a ridiculous thought, for he had probably undressed dozens of women over his lifetime, in much more passionate circumstances — he would hardly find the removal of a pair of gloves exciting in comparison.

"Mr Dubois said that he was in Truro in the weeks before my father's death," Hestia said, breaking the silence that had fallen between them. She tugged her hand away from his and began to pace the chequered tiles of the entrance hall. "Do you think Dubois could have killed him?"

"Dubois?" Falconbridge gave a bark of laughter. "He wouldn't be capable of anything like that."

"How do you know?" Hestia rounded on him, furious that he wasn't taking her seriously. "He seemed obsessed by the ruddy thing, from what I saw. Perhaps in a moment of madness, when my father would not give up his secrets, Mr Dubois just snapped?"

She clicked her fingers in a most un-ladylike fashion to emphasise her point, ignoring the look of incredulity on Falconbridge's handsome face.

"Did you know that he had gone to Truro?" she asked.

"He said he was going for a week to Cornwall to visit friends," the Marquess confessed.

"So he hid the fact that he went there from you?" she asked pointedly; that was a *most* illuminating piece of information. Why would Dubois not tell his colleague that he had tried to find the stone, unless he had something to hide?

"I think you are being ridiculous," Falconbridge replied, rather pompously, as she finished speaking. "I know Pierre Dubois, I have worked with him for years. The man is not capable of murder. In fact, he's not capable of buttoning his own shirt without the help of a valet. He did not kill your father, believe me."

"That's the second time today, that you've asked me to put my faith in your honesty, my Lord," Hestia retorted. "And you have put no faith whatsoever in my suspicions. If you'll excuse me, I must go upstairs and rest."

"I shall be here all evening," he called after her.

"And I shall be in my room all evening," Hestia replied, "*Believe me.*"

12 CHAPTER TWELVE

One's wedding was supposed to be a joyous occasion, but Hestia Stockbow wore an expression more suited to a funeral, as she exchanged vows with Alex.

The girl had not spoken to him properly since that disastrous afternoon, nearly a week before, when he had roundly dismissed her suspicions that Dubois had killed her father. Alex knew that he had been right in his beliefs, but he reluctantly conceded that could have been a tad more tactful in the way he had responded. Hestia had every right to be annoyed with him, and he was longing to apologise, but the stubborn woman had steadfastly avoided being alone with him, and so he had not had the opportunity to say sorry.

That would end today though, he thought with relief, there was no way that she could continue ignoring him once they were wed.

The wedding was a simple affair; the pair exchanged vows in the morning room of Thackery House, with Phoebe, the Earl and the newlywed Lord and Lady Payne present. Hestia was resplendent in a gown of pale, butter yellow that complimented her colouring. Alex thought fondly on her old, yellow ribboned bonnet, which he had not seen for a while, and decided that the colour suited his wife to perfection. He would commission a *modiste* to make her a dozen dresses all in varying shades, he decided.

Once the Vicar pronounced them married, the party retired to the dining room, where a breakfast buffet was laid out. Hestia took a seat beside Alex and silently began to eat her trout and eggs, as though he were not there.

"Are you going to ignore me forever?" Alex whispered, a little aggrieved that his new bride was so obviously underwhelmed by him.

"That depends. Are you going to continue to ignore me?" she asked calmly, placing her knife and fork down. "I told you that I believed my father was murdered, and you promised to help me find the perpetrator. Then you completely dismissed me when I presented you with a suspect who had means and motive."

Means and motive? Goodness, what type of ridiculous novels was she reading?

"I dismissed your claims because I know Dubois and I know that I am right in saying he did not kill your father," Alex tried to keep his voice low.

"Though perhaps I was a bit rude in the way that I explained myself. As for ignoring your suspicions that foul play was involved in your father's death, quite the opposite is true. I have arranged for us to honeymoon in Cornwall, where we can investigate the matter properly."

"We are going to Cornwall?"

Finally his new wife met his eye and he was left almost speechless by her beauty. Her huge, blue eyes were filled with hope and her plump mouth was parted as she awaited his reply. Alex had never seen her look so beautiful, and he wished that he had not promised her that he would wait until she was ready, to consummate the marriage.

"Yes, we will leave once breakfast has finished," he said casually. "I have a small estate near Penzance, though, obviously, we shall visit Truro first to begin our investigations."

"Oh, thank you, my Lord!" Hestia squealed, her face wreathed in a smile.

"For Heaven's sake, you're my wife now, call me Alex."

"Thank you, Alex," she repeated softly, offering him a shy smile that melted his heart. He had never heard a sweeter sound than his name on her lips.

Once breakfast had finished, and the newlyweds had said their goodbyes, Alex, Hestia and Henry all clambered in to the Marquess's well-sprung carriage. He tried to hide his surprise as the footman helped a fourth person inside —Hestia's flame haired lady's maid, Catherine.

His visions of he and his new wife sharing a tender moment instantly vanished; it seemed that Hestia too had realised the romantic opportunities a carriage ride might present, and had decided to put an obstacle in the way. Catherine was a pleasant girl, if a little talkative by the usual servant's standards. She and Hestia chatted easily for the duration of the journey, sharing an easy friendship that Alex was actually quite envious of.

As darkness fell, they stopped at a Coaching Inn, just outside of Alton, to rest for the night. Their bags and Alex's trusty valet, Thomas, had followed in a carriage behind them.

The proprietor of the inn fawned over the Marquess and his new bride, showing them to what he promised was his best room. Alex tried not to visibly grimace when the door opened to reveal a rather basic, but mercifully clean, room, with a large double bed and what looked like, he hoped, a feather mattress.

"Will my Lord and Lady be taking supper?" the inn-keeper asked hopefully.

"Yes, after we freshen up," Alex said with a nod. "Please have someone bring up some hot water for my wife."

My wife; the words felt natural as they rolled off his tongue.

The inn keeper nodded, gave a ridiculously elaborate bow and hurried off to fetch the bathwater. The door closed behind him with a sharp click, and Alex gave a happy sigh; finally he was alone with Hestia.

"How do you feel after the journey?" he asked.

She was standing by the window, with her back to him, staring out into the yard below.

"Quite well," she chirped, like a startled bird. His new wife was fidgeting with the sleeve of her dress, plucking the material in an absent minded, anxious way.

She's nervous, he realised with a jolt. Of course she was nervous, he could have cursed his thoughtlessness. Hestia was but twenty years of age, a young woman who had led, by all accounts, a sheltered life. Heaven knew what she thought might happen tonight, or what grisly tales of the marriage bed she had heard.

"When I said that I would not take you, until you were ready, I meant it," he said quietly, speaking across the distance between them. "Do not fear me, I'm not about to ravish you."

Never had he witnessed a woman flush so quickly; Hestia's cheeks were so red that if he had touched them, he thought they might scald him.

"Excuse my directness," he continued with an amused laugh at her obvious embarrassment, "We are married now, we can speak to each other openly about such things."

"Do you mind?" she ventured, turning to look at him, "Waiting?"

"I can't say I'll enjoy it," he grumbled in good-natured way, "But I won't be waiting too long...believe me."

Her eyes narrowed and the corners of her mouth quirked at his assured statement, he knew her well enough now, to know that she would try to resist the challenge —if only to prove him wrong.

"Pray tell, husband dear, how can you be so confident?"

"Your eyes give your true feelings away," he replied easily, crossing the room in three long strides so that he was standing before her. He cupped her chin in his hand and tilted her face up, so that she had nowhere to look but at him.

"You can't hide desire, Hestia," he whispered softly, "Not with eyes as expressive as yours."

Before she had a chance to protest that she felt no such thing, Alex dropped his lips to hers in a soft, tender kiss. The moment their lips connected, she melted against him, thus proving his point perfectly. His lips, which were still on hers, curled into a triumphant smile, which she seemed to feel, for she pulled away defiantly.

"That's not fair," she protested, thwacking his chest with her hand. "You took me by surprise, and besides, you have far more experience than I at this!"

"And that's the way it shall stay," he whispered possessively, "You won't be gaining experience with anyone but me."

His lips claimed hers again in a kiss that was far more passionate than the last, perhaps it would have progressed further but a knock on the door jolted them apart.

"I shall call for Catherine to assist you," Alex said, in voice that was hoarse with desire, as a chamber-maid carried a steaming bucket of water inside. He ran a distracted hand through his hair and went in search of Hestia's lady's maid. His wife was right when she had said that he had far more experience than she, though he had never experienced a passion like this in all   his   life.

"Tell me about the night your father died," Alex said, later that evening when they had finished dining. They were seated in a small parlour of the inn, which afforded them the privacy needed to discuss David Stockbow's apparent murder.

In a halting voice, that occasionally shook with emotion, Hestia laid out the facts of the matter.

"Have you any idea who the blonde haired man, that your father saw, might be?" Alex asked, once his wife had finished speaking.

"I'm rather inclined to think it was Dubois," she answered tartly, casting him a defiant look.

"And, as I have told you, I'm rather inclined to think that it wasn't," he dead-panned, scratching his chin thoughtfully.

"Your father made many enemies over his lifetime, all infinitely more dangerous than Pierre Dubois," he continued gently. "Can you think of anything else he might have stolen, that would cause someone to murder him in cold blood?"

"He always brought back things of value," Hestia replied with a shrug, reaching down to scoop Henry up into her lap. "Furs, jewels —things that could be pawned easily. There was never that much left by the time he reached England. I'm wont to think that in his latter years, he wasn't that adept at piracy."

"The world changed," Alex shrugged, "The Navy became better equipped during the war. Your father would have been a foolish man to try and take on any of Wellington's ships."

Indeed, toward the middle of the war, David Stockbow seemed to have disappeared from the seas, from what Alex knew. Captain Black, the young man to whom Stockbow had left his sword, had alluded that the pirate was engaged in other activities, but had point blank refused to divulge any more information when Alex had pressed him. It all left Alex feeling rather uncomfortable, for if Stockbow had been engaged in espionage for the French and it all came to light, then his new wife's reputation would never recover. She would be shunned completely by a society that had only just reluctantly accepted her.

"We will reach Truro by nightfall tomorrow," Alex said, as the inn-keeper brought him a tankard of ale. "I can have Thomas check the local taverns, to see if he can discover anything. People will be far more willing to talk to him than I."

That was because the people Thomas would be speaking to, would be thieves and ruffians, who had a natural mistrust of the aristocracy —though Alex wasn't about to tell his new bride that.

Once his pint was finished, the new bride and groom repaired to their bedroom. Alex gritted his teeth against the well wishes of the inn-keeper, who gave him a subtle, saucy wink as he passed. The man naturally believed that the Marquess was retiring to consummate his marriage, when the opposite was in fact true.

Hestia changed behind the screen, in the corner of the room, whilst Alex undressed easily by the wash-basin. She shuffled out, wearing a petrified look and a nightshift that fell to the floor.

"Don't look so frightened," Alex grumbled, as he quickly washed his chest with the cool water in the basin. "Did we not discuss tonight's activities earlier?"

"We did," Hestia nibbled her plump lip nervously, in a way that made Alex want to groan. "Though you did not mention activities at the time…"

"Well, my main activity will involve making a bed in the corner, that is comfortable enough to sleep on," Alex smiled, walking toward the actual bed and removing several woollen blankets. "Whilst yours will involved making yourself as cosy as possible on the feather mattress."

The look of relief on her face tugged at his heartstrings; his wife was not ready to become him, and despite his confident assurances to her that she would soon relent, doubt was starting to creep in.

"Goodnight Hestia," he said solemnly, as he threw his blankets over the armchair by the fireplace.

"Goodnight Alex," came her sleepy reply.

At least she was calling him by his given name, he thought as he settled himself down for the night, that was an improvement of sorts.

13 CHAPTER THIRTEEN

"Well, was I not right?"

"Right about what?"

"That leaving Cornwall would secure you a husband."

Hestia resisted rolling her eyes as Lady Bedford gave her a smug smile and glanced obviously at the Marquess, who was wrestling with a wriggling herd of Cavaliers in the corner of the room.

"I think you said, that if I stayed in Cornwall, I would never find a husband," Hestia responded, suppressing a grin. "Which is quite a different thing."

"Balderdash, I know what I said," Lady Bedford snorted, "And look at you now —a Marchioness!"

Although she was now officially titled the Marchioness of Falconbridge, she still felt like plain, old Hestia Stockbow. Even more so, now that she was seated before Lady Bedford, the woman who had so kindly seen her, and her mother, through years of genteel poverty.

"It still feels so strange," she confessed to the older woman, "I am so grateful to Lord Delaney for all the help that he has provided me."

"I'm sure he was more than grateful for the opportunity to help you," Lady Bedford raised her eyebrows, "Judging by the way he looks at you. He's smitten, and I don't blame him."

Hestia flushed at her kind words, wishing that she could tell Lady Bedford that Alex had only married her out of a misplaced sense of duty. She wasn't even a proper wife yet; she had not given him anything of herself. The memory of his muscular chest, as he had changed for bed the previous night, flashed across her mind's eye. He was so masculine, it was almost overwhelming. A part of her longed for him, but another part, the part that had witnessed the disaster her parent's passion for each other had caused, still resisted. Though one day,she knew, she would have to allow him his liberties.

She, Alex and Lady Bedford were taking breakfast together in the dining room. They had arrived at Bedford Hall the previous evening and had been shown to a bedroom far more luxurious than any Hestia had previously been permitted to stay in. Henry had abandoned his mistress, in favour of his siblings, and so Hestia had slept alone in the huge, four-poster bed, extremely conscious of the Marquess, who had slumbered, again, in a chair by the fireplace.

"Trout, Lord Delaney?" Lady Bedford called, as the servants arrived with plates of food.

The maids and footmen threw Hestia subtle glances as they laid the breakfast on the table, no doubt amazed that the girl who used to come begging, now held a higher title than their mistress.

"I was just thinking of trout," Alex called innocently, as he abandoned the dogs and took a seat at the table. Hestia suppressed a laugh, knowing he was making fun of Lady Bedford, who could be a tad overbearing.

The trio discussed the activities for the day, with Lord Delaney calmly supplying Lady Bedford with a false itinerary. Once breakfast had ended, she and Alex rescued Henry from a fight that had broken out between all the dogs and left for the short walk to Rose Cottage.

"Your father bequeathed the house to you, in his will," Alex said, as they made their way down the quiet lane way, towards Hestia's former home.

"Did he leave many possessions?" she asked calmly, hoping that Alex could not tell that the calmness was a front. She knew that her face was drawn and her shoulders stiff, despite her best efforts. The prospect of returning to the place that her father had been murdered, was taking more of a toll than she had imagined.

"Not many," he replied cautiously, picking up a stick and tossing it for Henry. The Cavalier threw him a rather superior look, as if to say "Fetch that yourself" and continued trotting slowly beside his mistress.

"He did leave a sword to a man called Captain Black," Falconbridge added casually, then waited for her response, as though he expected her to recognise the name.

"Captain Who?" she questioned, her pace slowing, "Is he another privateer?"

"No, actually, he was a Navy Captain —and a well regarded one at that," Alex added, which made Hestia frown. Why had her father bequeathed a Navy man his sword? It made no sense.

"This is it," Hestia stated, as they reached a small, tumbledown cottage. It had a thatched roof, which sagged in the middle, and was enclosed by a low stone wall, parts of which had fallen into disrepair.

"The winter winds can be very cruel here," Hestia said absently, trailing a hand along the wall. She felt slightly defensive of her home, even though she knew it must appear terribly run-down to a lofty Marquess.

"How charming," her new husband said, his eyes raking over the garden where dozens of early spring flowers grew. "It is most quaint. I can imagine you were very happy here as a child."

"I was," she replied, pushing the gate, which was stiff from disuse, open and strolling up the garden path to the front door. It was locked, though the key which was hidden in a plant-pot, still worked. Hestia pushed the door open, braced herself and stepped inside.

"Oh," she said aloud, as she saw the dust-covered kitchen was the same as it had been the last time she was there. She had expected, perhaps, to find signs of a struggle, or even bloodstains, but mercifully all she found was a room filled with memories.

"Is everything alright?" Alex asked, his face a picture of concern.

"I had just expected..." Hestia trailed off, unsure of what she wanted to say, or how to respond to his question. Everything was not alright; her parents were gone and she was all alone in the world.

A pair of strong arms wrapped around her, and to her surprise she found herself cradled against the Marquess's strong chest.

"There, there," he said, stroking her hair tenderly, "It's alright to cry."

She hadn't even realised that she was crying, but once he had said the words, she felt the tears which stained her cheeks. He held her tightly, as sob after sob wracked her body, never once letting her go, or complaining about his shirt, which was quickly ruined by her tears.

"I am sorry," she whispered, once she had regained her composure, "I don't know what came over me."

"Grief," he responded quietly, "And please, don't apologise for it."

Hestia ran her hands down her dress, smoothing her skirts which had become wrinkled, and nodded her head. She wanted to thank him for his kindness, but she did not trust her voice not to falter. Just when she had thought herself alone, he had proved her wrong, and the thought was both comforting and a little unsettling.

It would be so easy to fall in love with the brooding man standing opposite her, though her head was quick to overrule her heart. Love brought nothing but trouble, she reminded herself, thinking on how unhappy her mother's final months had been.

"Shall we have a look around?" she suggested brightly, once she was certain that she would not collapse again, into floods of tears. The pair spent an hour rifling through cupboards and drawers, seeking some kind of clue, but they found nothing.

"It's hopeless," she said, sadly. "The original letter has long since disappeared, we will find nothing here, I know it."

"I'm afraid I have to agree," Alex said with a sigh, taking a seat at the old, wooden kitchen table. "Your father was not overly fond of keeping written records."

"What about this Captain Black fellow?" Hestia asked desperately. "If my father knew him well enough to have left him a sword, then perhaps he might know something that we don't."

The Marquess scratched his chin thoughtfully, nodding his head in agreement with her.

"The fellow is employed by the Duke of Everleigh," he said, "He captains one of his many ships. Perhaps we shall pay a visit to Pemberton, as a detour on the way to Penzance, and see if the Duke knows of Black's current whereabouts."

Pemberton, the Duke's Cornwall estate, was located a few miles outside of St Jarvis. It was most definitely not a "detour" from the route they would have travelled to Penzance, but rather about one hundred miles in the opposite direction.

"Thank you," Hestia said solemnly, hoping that her husband would see the gratitude in her eyes. "If I can be so bold as to ask you one more favour?"

"Anything."

"I would like to visit the place where my father is buried."

A look of alarm passed over her husband's face, though to his credit he quickly hid it.

"If that is what you wish," he said, standing up and stretching lightly, "Then that is what we shall do."

They left the cottage, locking the door behind them. Just before Hestia reached the gate, she remembered the roses that her father had planted for her mother, in his strange rockery at the side of the house.

"One moment," she whispered, picking up her skirts and making her way across the grass. There were few flowers on the rose bushes, as it was too early in the season, but those that were there Hestia took. Once she had picked enough to make a bunch that wasn't too pathetic looking, she made her way back to where Alex was waiting for her.

"Are you alright?" he asked, as he offered her his arm.

"Much better," she decided, slipping her arm through his and allowing him to lead the way.

Truro was often called the London of Cornwall —and for good reason. The carriage which brought Hestia and her husband to her father's final resting place, made its way down Walsingham Place then on to Lemon Street, where the townhouses were so fine as to rival Bath.

As they travelled further out, through warrens of close, cobblestone streets, the architecture of the houses became far less impressive. The graveyard was located on a road which led to one of the nearby tin mines. It was a dark, country road —though one could still see the spires of St. Mary's, which gave Hestia a little relief.

"'Lo, 'lo," an old, wizened man said, shuffling forward to greet Hestia and the Marquess as they alighted the carriage. "Been told to meet yer here, m'lord, m'lady. I's Jim."

The man gave an arthritic bow, that Hestia momentarily feared he may not rise from, before breaking out into a gap-toothed smile.

"I ain't never had a Marquess and a March—march...and 'is wife visiting me a'fore."

"Well," Alex had adopted the brusque manner of a titled man, "As they say, Jim, there is a first time for everything."

Hestia pretended not to notice as her husband discreetly slipped a few coins into the old man's palm. The weight of the coins in his pocket seemed to lift old Jim's spirits, for he gave an even larger grin and began to shuffle quickly into the deserted graveyard.

"Yer father is down t'back, where most of t'new lads are buried," he called, leading Hestia and Alex through the twilight. The ground was uneven and Hestia tripped once or twice, only realising afterward that what she had tripped over were the mounds of earth where men lay buried.

"How do you remember who is who?" she asked, quelling the bile that was rising in her throat. There were no headstones or markers on the graves to distinguish who was buried beneath.

"I keep the name of every soul that lies in these grounds up here," the gravedigger said, pointing his finger to his head, which was covered by a mere wisp of grey hair. "I recite alls their names a'fore I fall asleep, say a prayer for them like. I knows they were judged not worthy of a headstone, but only the good Lord has the right to judge. Every soul deserves a prayer, is what I think."

Hot tears pricked Hestia's eyes at the man's simple words, and she felt a rush of gratitude to him for his compassion. It soothed her soul to think that there was someone else in the world, who cared enough to pray for her father.

"'Ere 'e is," Jim said, with little ceremony, as they reached a place where the earth still had the look of being recently disturbed. "I'll leave you alone for a moment."

Hestia stared down at the ground where her father lay buried, blinking back tears from her eyes. It was such a bleak, lonely spot —not a place he would have chosen, had he a choice.

"These are for you, father," she whispered, placing the bunch of flowers down on the mound of earth. She stood in silence, for how long she did not know, until she felt a strong hand take hers.

"You're shaking."

It was Alex, his voice low and deep with concern. Hestia had not noticed, but once he said it, she realised he was right. Her whole body trembled with a deep cold that seemed to have seeped into her very bones. She allowed her husband to lead her away, past Jim —whom he thanked—and back to the carriage.

She did not remember the journey from Truro to Bedford Hall, though she did remember the feeling of safety as her husband carried her bodily from the carriage and up the stairs to her bed chambers.

Alex removed her shoes and her outer garments, before placing her gently in her bed.

"Don't leave me," she whispered, though she was almost afraid of the sheer need she felt for the strength that his presence gave her.

"Never," was his gentle reply.

He lay down, still clothed, beside her and drew her to his chest. He stroked her back as she shed a thousand tears, and when she awoke in the morning, she was still wrapped in his arms, and nothing had ever felt so right.

14 CHAPTER FOURTEEN

Alex arrived in St Jarvis, hopeful that something there might lead to more clues about David Stockbow's life and death —because after Truro, he was beginning to think that Hestia was right in suspecting Dubois.

Thomas had made enquiries in Truro's less salubrious inns, and had learned that Dubois had indeed been spotted there the week before Stockbow's murder. The local ruffians had been reluctant to give the London valet much more information, but they had hinted that Dubois had been seeking the services of hired muscle.

Perhaps Alex had been right when he said that Dubois was far too lazy to murder a man —though it was beginning to appear that he was capable of hiring someone else to carry out the act.

The Marquess had not shared his growing sense of unease with his new bride, preferring instead to make for St Jarvis. He was certain that this Captain Black would reveal a missing piece of the puzzle—he just had to find him.

"Do you know the Duke of Everleigh well?" Hestia asked, as their carriage made its way slowly up the drive of Pemberton Hall, the Duke's Cornish residence.

"Well enough," Alex shrugged, which was to say not that well at all. Though few could claim a close acquaintance with the Duke, who was infamous for shunning society. He had written ahead, to inform Everleigh of his purpose for visiting, so they were greeted quite cordially upon their arrival.

"How lovely to see you again," Olive, Duchess of Everleigh said with a genuinely warm smile as she embraced Hestia in a warm hug. "Ruan is out riding, though if you come through to the parlour, you'll find a surprise guest to greet you."

"Jane!"

Hestia appeared overjoyed to find the new Lady Payne waiting patiently in the elegant parlour room, at the front of the house. Alex watched, overcome with jealousy as his wife's eyes lit up at the sight of her friend. Would his new Marchioness ever greet him with that same excitement?

"You look marvellous," Lady Payne cried, holding Hestia at arm's length, so that she could inspect her properly. Hestia was dressed in a simple riding gown of emerald green, made from warm but fine wool. On her ears she wore dark ruby earrings, a parting gift from Lady Phoebe and on her finger was a large emerald ring that Alex had given her on their wedding day.

"As do you," Hestia replied, and Alex had to agree— for Jane was blooming. Her cheeks were rosy against her alabaster skin and her luscious brunette hair was gleaming.

"The countryside suits me," Jane laughed modestly, gesturing for them both to sit. They were joined by Olive, who was ushering a maid inside to serve tea.

Once everyone was served and they had exchanged pleasantries, the topic of conversation changed to London, and the goings on of the ton.

"Well, I know you will be loathe to hear this, but everyone has stopped talking about your marriage," Jane said with a laugh, "They have now settled on discussing the fact that the Viscount Havisham has taken to the drink, and that the Duke of Morhaven is missing his new bride."

"How did Morhaven manage to lose his new wife?" Alex asked, with an amused laugh, not wanting to discuss Hestia's uncle's drinking habits on such a pleasant afternoon.

"It's easily done, I assure you."

The Duke of Everleigh had arrived, his face watching his wife with unconcealed affection. Olive had flushed at his joke, for it was well known that she had fled to Cornwall after marrying Everleigh, thinking him a murderer and a cad.

"Apparently the girl, who's Irish, didn't want to marry him in the first place," Jane continued as Everleigh sat down to join them. "I can't say I blame her; Morhaven has always been a charlatan."

"He's not so bad, if you approach him with a bellyful of brandy," Everleigh shrugged, glancing at Alex surreptitiously. The Marquess instantly picked up on the Duke's subtle hint, and both men excused themselves for a visit to the library.

"How are you finding married life?" Everleigh asked, as he handed Alex a tumbler of brandy. The Marquess shrugged, thinking how best to answer. What would the Duke say if he confessed that he had found the past week a mixture of pure joy and agonising torture? Sharing a bed chamber with a bride who had no interest in you, was much more difficult than he had ever imagined.

"Well enough," he replied, "A little tiring, but nothing a good night's sleep won't sort."

The Duke's raised eyebrows and snort of amusement, reminded Alex that no one —bar he and Hestia—knew that their marriage remained, as yet, unconsummated.

"Thank you for your hospitality, Everleigh," Alex blustered, the tips of his ears a little red from his unintended innuendo. "It's mighty sporting of you."

"Her Grace adores company," Everleigh replied with a small nod of his head.

"And you?"

"Depends on the visitor, Falconbridge," the Duke laughed, his teeth flashing white against his tanned skin. Alex knew that, like himself, the Duke was a man who preferred to be out of doors, and it showed. "I shall enjoy yours, never fear. Now, tell me, what business do you have with my Captain Black?"

"If I'm honest, I don't actually know," Alex confessed. He relayed the tale of Hestia's father's will and the surprise association that David Stockbow had had with the young Black.

"He was in the Navy for a time," the Duke said, scratching his chin thoughtfully, "That much I know. He's a quiet fellow, doesn't give much away, but I know him to be an honest, trustworthy sort."

"I thought the same," Alex shrugged, "And loyal. He did say that he owed Stockbow his life and a man like Black would take that debt most seriously. Perhaps, however, if…"

"If it was Stockbow's daughter asking him to give up his secrets?" Everleigh finished for him, with a wry smile. "He is most chivalrous. I'm certain when he arrives, that he will be very accommodating to Lady Delaney."

"He is on his way?" Alex hadn't expected the Duke to summon Black until Everleigh had heard why Alex was so desperate to meet with him.

"I asked Olive her opinion on the matter," Everleigh shrugged, "And as she holds your wife in such high esteem, she thought it was safe to send for him."

"My thanks to your wife," Alex inclined his head.

"Don't thank mine, thank yours," Everleigh responded, raising his glass in toast to both women.

After a late supper, Alex and Hestia joined Jane and the Duchess, in paying a visit to the boarding house in St Jarvis. It had once been run by an inimitable woman called Mrs Barker, who had set the guest house up as a sort of refuge for ladies with intellectual inclinations.

Today the proprietress was a Miss Polly Jenkins, a fiery red-head with a warm, Northern accent. Polly lived there with her sister and hosted a dozen ladies, ranging in age from eighteen to eighty.

On their previous visit, Alex had been too agitated to appreciate Polly's charming, direct manner, or the easy, warm atmosphere of the guest-house. When they arrived the drawing room was filled with ladies, waiting patiently for a reading of Mrs Actrol's latest Gothic Romance. Polly ushered Alex and Hestia into a small sofa, so tiny, that they were squashed together side by side.

"I'll fetch you both some tea," she beamed, bustling away, only to return moments later with two china cups for them. "There you go, my Lord, my Lady. Don't drink too quickly; Mrs Actrol does love the sound of her own voice, so you'll be here a while."

"Poppycock," Mrs Actrol, who had overheard, blustered. "I only read for so long, because the ladies insist that I do."

Indeed, once the authoress began her reading, the ladies of the boarding house fell silent, listening with rapt attention, to what Alex thought was a rather preposterous tale.

"Imagine a man deciding to marry a woman he had won at cards," Alex scoffed quietly to Hestia, who giggled at his outrage.

"You don't have to imagine," she whispered, glancing at Olive, "For you're sitting right opposite her."

Oh, he had quite forgotten that Everleigh had tricked Olive's father into gambling away her hand in marriage. He glanced surreptitiously at Mrs Actrol, who for all intents and purposes looked like an innocent grandmother, and hoped that she would not find inspiration for another tale in his own marriage.

The room was silent, as the guests listened to Mrs Actrol read the end of the chapter. It was so quiet, that when a loud rapping came upon the front door, several of the guests jumped.

"My, who could that be at this hour?" Polly grumbled, making to stand up.

"Allow me, Miss Jenkins."

As the sole male in attendance, and with night having fallen, Alex felt that he should be the one to answer the impatient caller, who had continued rapping.

"Hold your horses," he called, making his way down the hallway to the door, which he threw open in irritation.

The man standing on the doorstep was none other than Captain Black, drenched to the bone from the rain, which was lashing in off the Cornish coast.

"My apologies for the noise," he said with a smile as his teeth chattered, "But His Grace told me that you needed me urgently."

"You look like you need a cup of tea urgently, Captain," Alex replied, standing aside so that Black could step in out of the rain. "The ladies are in the parlour, and I'm loathe to interrupt their enjoyment of the evening. I'm sure between the two of us we can find the kitchen and boil a kettle."

The two men made their way back down the hallway, passing the parlour where Alex could still hear Mrs Actrol's booming voice as she read. The door opened and Emily, Polly's sister, poked her head out, a smile on her innocent face.

"The kitchen?" Alex whispered gently.

Emily pointed shyly down the corridor, apparently afraid of speaking in front of two strange men. Her wide eyes caught sight of Captain Black and her mouth opened into an "O" of surprise.

"My friend has come to visit," Alex whispered, gesturing to Black, who stood somewhat in the shadows. "Would you be so kind as to tell my wife that she is needed in the kitchen?"

The young woman nodded and disappeared, leaving Alex to lead Black in the direction that Emily had pointed in.

"The proprietress's younger sister," Alex said by way of explanation, for it had been too dark for the Captain to see the girl clearly. "She's a rather special young woman, I am told."

Daft, was the word that some people would have used to describe Emily, or soft-headed. Both expressions left a rather bitter taste in Alex's mouth, for Emily was as he had described; special, unique and innocent.

The kitchen was an enormous, flag-stoned room, with a huge wood-burning stove that threw off great heat. Alex dragged a chair over to beside the stove, insisting that Captain Black dry off before they discussed anything.

"Thank you, my Lord," the young man laughed, "But I'm well acquainted with being soaked to the bone —perils of the occupation, as you well understand."

"You're off duty now," Alex reminded him, "You have every right to be dry. Sit down and I'll fetch you some tea."

The kitchen was not a room that Alex would consider his area of expertise, though he managed to make the young Captain a cup of tea without causing too much mess. The Captain took the cup with thanks and Alex noted that, while his clothes were as fine as any gentleman's, the Captain had the hands of a man who worked.

The door opened and Hestia slipped into the room, just as Alex was taking a seat.

"My dear," he said, standing again at the sight of his wife, "This is Captain Black, your father's old friend. Captain Black, I'd like to introduce you to my wife, the Marchioness of Falconbridge."

"A pleasure, my Lady" Black, who had also stood on Hestia's arrival gave a bow. If he was shocked that the man he had met less than a month ago, had gone on to marry the ward that he had proclaimed he did not want, the Captain's handsome face hid it well.

"I take it then, that your business with me is related to the late David Stockbow?" Black asked, once a chair had been fetched for Hestia.

"You would be right," Alex leaned forward, watching the Captain closely for any signs of unease. He saw none, Black seemed relaxed, he wore the look of a man anticipating a friendly conversation, rather than an inquisition.

"Did you know my father well, Captain?"

Hestia was the first to speak, her face bright with hope. Alex felt a wrenching in his gut; he did not want his wife to hear anything bad said against her father, but he feared the worst. Worse still, it had to be done— for they would never solve the mystery of Stockbow's death, unless they understood how he had lived the last years of his life.

"I knew him a little," the Captain cleared his throat nervously, as he addressed the Marchioness. "For the first few years of my apprenticeship in the Navy, your father was quite the legend. In fact, he attacked the first ship I ever sailed on."

"Oh, dear," Hestia chewed her lip nervously, evidently unhappy at this news.

"No," the Captain laughed easily, "Don't be upset. He was quite gallant. In fact he saved my life. A few of us young tars had ignored our Captain's instructions to surrender. I soon found myself with a knife against my throat, and only for your father's interrupting my would-be killer, I would not be here to tell the tale."

This seemed to mollify Hestia, and the look of distress left her face. Alex frowned; he knew that he needed to question Black on Stockbow's activities during the war, but feared that Hestia's relief would be short-lived if he did.

"Did you ever meet him again, after that?" Hestia asked, interrupting Alex's train of thought.

"I did," the Captain was solemn now. He sighed deeply, as though weighing his words before he spoke them. "During the war your father acted as a spy for the British —it was easy for him to convince the French that he had little interest in a British Victory."

Alex looked up, startled by this turn of events. He had thought Stockbow a traitor; a stab of guilt pierced his heart. He had been so quick to judge the man, because he had been a pirate, but even thieves had honour, it seemed.

"He carried messages, wounded soldiers, even arms, across the channel. It was quite risky," Black continued, "In fact, one of Napoleon's ships attacked him near Calais, just before war's end. It was lucky that my men and I happened upon the fighting. We managed to see the French off, and your father was able to transfer two-dozen infantry men, who were being returned home, safely to my ship."

"So he was a hero?" Hestia whispered, her eyes shining brightly.

"Of sorts, though he made me swear upon my life, to never tell a soul." Black laughed, a deep rumble that filled the room. With his dark black hair, tanned skin and the wicked glint in his eye, the young Captain looked momentarily like a pirate himself.

"He worked for England, but still reserved the right to pilfer as he pleased," Black looked deeply amused at this, "And the government allowed him— Whitehall were grateful for any help they could get, at the time."

"Can you think of anyone, anyone at all, that Stockbow might have crossed during his tenure for the Crown?" Alex asked. That David Stockbow had turned out to be a hero, of sorts, was heartening for his wife, but not for their investigation.

"I can't say," Black replied, shaking his head. "Stockbow was a thief, but he was known for always behaving with honour when he attacked a ship. There is no one, that I know of, who held a deep grudge against him."

Alex stifled a sigh; they were back to square one. Though the happiness in his wife's eyes was heartening, he felt a rising despair at the thought that Dubois might actually be guilty of murder.

The sound of the ladies leaving the parlour and traipsing up the stairs, all achatter, jolted the trio from their conversation.

"I had not realised the time," Captain Black said, rising to stand. "It was a pleasure to meet you again, my Lord."

"Do you have somewhere to stay for the night?" Alex questioned, he didn't want the poor chap sleeping out in the rain.

"I'll stay here, I think, if there's a bed," Black shrugged, nonchalant.

"I'm sure there's a room in Pemberton Hall, though if you desire to stay close to the town, I'm certain that Polly will put you up."

"Polly?"

Was it Alex's imagination, or had the young man turned pale at the name?

"Yes, Polly Jenkins. She runs the boarding house," Alex replied, a little concerned that Black's relaxed demeanour had changed so suddenly.

"And the girl?" the Captain's voice was hoarse, "The young girl from earlier?"

"Who? Oh, Emily; why she's Polly's sister, as I already told you."

Captain Black's mouth was a grim line, as he nodded his head.

"Thank you, my Lord," he said, rising to stand. "I shall go find this Miss Jenkins and beg a room for the night."

With a curt bow, the Captain left, leaving a rather bemused Alex and a tired Hestia in the kitchen.

"Shall we return to Pemberton?" Alex asked gently; his wife's eyes were heavy with sleep. He couldn't blame her —it had been an evening of revelations. His own mind was still attempting to digest the idea that a man he had worked with, for years, was capable of murder. Added to this was the guilt that he had not yet shared his suspicions with Hestia; though admitting that he thought Dubois guilty, was as good as signing the man's death warrant.

"Yes. I fear we have outstayed our welcome —it sounds like everyone has gone to bed."

Hestia allowed him to take her hand, and assist her from her chair. As she stood, she stumbled, falling against his chest. Her scent, a soft mixture of sweet florals, threatened to overwhelm him. He dropped his head, to place a chaste kiss upon her lips, but was met by an eagerness that soon turned the tender embrace rather more passionate.

"Thank you, for everything, Alex," Hestia whispered, as they broke apart. Her eyes were bright, shining with happiness as she looked up at him. "I don't know how to express how much all this means to me, except—"
She broke off and flushed, turning her face away from his shyly.

"Except what?" he asked, a little befuddled by her sudden embarrassment.

His wife went up on her tip-toes, to place a kiss on his lips. The first kiss offered and not stolen, he thought as he realised exactly how his wife wished to express her gratitude. Within his chest a lion roared victory and his body stirred at the thought of how he might finally make her his proper wife.

Though, how could he claim to be a proper husband, if he was not telling her the whole truth? Inside his head a battle raged between his conscience and his body —and he was not entirely certain who would win.

"Let's go home," he said, a little gruffly, taking her hand and leading her to the waiting carriage that would take them back to Pemberton.

15 CHAPTER FIFTEEN

In all her life, Hestia had never felt so humiliated.

"Slow down, my lady," Catherine called from behind her, as they raced along the rugged cliffs by Pemberton Hall. "Even Henry can't keep up!"

Indeed, poor Henry was looking a little tired, as he moved his short legs as quickly as possible to keep up with them.

"I'm sorry," Hestia cried, coming to an abrupt halt. So abrupt, that Catherine thusly ran into her.

"Whatever's the matter, my Lady?" the girl asked, in her gentle lilt, as she saw the tears on Hestia's cheeks.

She could not tell Catherine what was bothering her, no matter how kind the girl's intentions, for it was too humiliating to bear. Last night, she had offered herself to her husband, only to have her overtures coldly refused.

The moment that she had invited Alex to share her bed, his face had taken on a strange expression and he had wordlessly shook his head in response.

"I shall remain on the floor tonight, my dear," he had said, through clenched teeth. Hestia, who after all their passionate kisses, had been expecting a rather warmer response, had nearly died of mortification. She had lain in the bed, stiff as poker, willing the silent tears of shame to stop, before her new husband heard and realised how much he had upset her.

That morning she had decided to be as cold as he, and had refused his offer of visiting St Jarvis, instead opting to walk along the cliffs.

"Something's the matter, my Lady," Catherine said gently, reaching into the pocket of her skirt and extracting a handkerchief. She passed it to Hestia, who noted the initials "RBM" embroidered in the corner, before she patted the tears from her cheeks. She wondered idly, who this RBM might be, but did not dare ask, in case it was a previous suitor of Catherine's.

"Thank you, Catherine," she said, passing the cotton cloth back to her waiting maid. The wind rustled her skirts and Hestia felt soft droplets of salty rain.

"Oh, dear," she sighed, glancing up at the sky. A huge bank of grey clouds could be seen, rolling in from across the sea.

"Looks like the Irish are sending over the rain," Catherine said with a smile, "Perhaps it would be best to return to Pemberton, my Lady? I'm not sure that Henry would appreciate getting soaked."

Hestia glanced down at her faithful companion, who had thrown himself miserably upon the grass. He looked up at her, his brown eyes pleading and she relented.

"You're quite right, Catherine," she replied in a brisk voice, hoping to gain some composure over her feelings. "We shall return to Pemberton, post haste."

As they walked, at a much more relaxed pace than before, the two women fell into easy conversation.

"One of the scullery maids said this morning that there was a terrible commotion last night," Catherine confided, "A man called Captain Black arrived, he works for the Duke on one of his ships. Well, the proprietress of the boarding house refused him a room, and he had to walk all the way from St Jarvis to Pemberton, by foot in the rain."

Hestia digested this news silently, recalling the Captain's strange behaviour the previous night, when he had learned Polly's name. The two evidently knew each other; though if Polly had refused Black a room for the night, then she clearly wasn't overly fond of the Captain. Which was a surprise, for Hestia had found the handsome Captain most charming and unassuming.

There was nobody home when the pair arrived back from their walk, bar the staff who bustled to and fro. Hestia went to her suite of rooms, hoping that perhaps Alex would be there, so that they could discuss what had happened the previous night. He was nowhere to be found however, and, thinking that she did not want to spend a dull afternoon alone, Hestia went in search of the library and a good book.

Pemberton Hall, which Olive had told her had originally been built in the fourteenth century, was a warren of corridors. It took Hestia a quarter of an hour to find the library, though when she pushed the door open a crack, she paused at the sound of a familiar voice.

"I'm blasted if I know what to do Everleigh."

It was Alex, and by the sounds of it he was pacing back and forth. Despite knowing that she should not be eavesdropping on her husband's conversations, Hestia paused, wondering if perhaps he was discussing his marriage. Hopefully he and the Duke weren't so close that he would share the diabolical scene from last night; Hestia flushed, that would truly be adding insult to injury.

"It's a tricky situation, I agree," the Duke replied, in a very serious voice. "Are you certain that Dubois is guilty?"

"I am, now. I did not want to believe it, but after what Thomas found out in Truro —that there were witnesses to say Dubois had tried to hire men to attack Stockbow…"

Alex trailed off, whilst Hestia stifled a gasp of shock and incredulity. Her husband had known since Truro that Dubois was most certainly her father's killer, and yet had not bothered to tell her.

"What shall you do?" Everleigh asked gravely.

Hestia waited for Alex to respond with a suitable answer; preferably along the lines of hanging and quartering this criminal Dubois. Instead, her husband heaved a huge sigh, and simply stated "I don't know."

She took a step back from the door, shocked by his ambivalent reply. How could he not know what to do? Was it easy for him to overlook his friend's guilt, simply because her father had been a criminal?

"Did you hear something?" Alex asked sharply from inside. Panic surged in Hestia's chest; she could not face him now. She turned and fled the way she had come, never once glancing behind her to see if he was following.

When she reached the entrance hall, the front door was open. She could see the sun shining outside and longed for some fresh air, to help her breathing, which was coming in short, sharp bursts.

That scoundrel, she thought furiously, as she tripped lightly down the wide steps onto the driveway. That blackguard; he promised that he would help me find the man who had killed my father and then he hid the perpetrator's identity from me purposefully.

She thought back to the previous night, when she had asked Alex solemnly to share her bed, and bile rose in her throat. Thank goodness he had refused, or she would surely have run him through with a sword, now that she knew what a lying, deceitful prig he had turned out to be.

Hestia was so furious that she was near running, and soon she had reached the end of the pebbled driveway. Thinking that she would walk into St Jarvis, and call on Jane, she walked out the wrought-iron gates and onto the country road which led to the town. She had been walking for no more than five minutes, when a farmer on a cart stopped to offer her a lift.

"Thank you, sir," she said gratefully, accepting his gnarled hand and sitting up beside him. "Are you going toward St Jarvis, by any chance?"

"I'll pass near enough, my love," the man said, with a wizened smile, "Thoughs I'll be staying on the main road to Truro."

"Oh. Perhaps I could beg a lift all the way there then, if it would not be too much trouble, sir?" Hestia replied impulsively. The urge to return home was overwhelming; she could not stay in Pemberton and look her husband in the eye, when she knew him to be such a cad. Truro was home, and Rose Cottage, though no doubt cold and damp, was hers.

"It's no trouble at all, Miss," the farmer replied jovially, flicking the reins so that the old-cart horse took off at a snail's pace, "In fact, I like having company on long drives. Tell me this; do you know much about growing turnips?"

"Nothing at all, sir," Hestia replied truthfully.

By the time they reached Truro, late that evening, just as darkness was falling, Hestia could have written an encyclopedia on the growing of root vegetables. She waved the farmer and his cart full of turnips goodbye under the watchful spires of St Mary's. He was headed west, toward Market Square, where he would sell his wares the next morning, whilst Hestia was going eastward toward home.

She made her way down the winding streets, past houses, which stood huddled atop each other, then cottages which stood apart, until finally she was walking along the familiar country lane, which would take her home. The last traces of light had just left the sky when she arrived at the gate of Rose Cottage. Her earlier anger at Alex had wiped any sensible thoughts from her mind, for she suddenly realised that she had no food, or even kindling to light a fire.

I feel as though there's something else I have forgotten, she thought idly, as she pushed the wooden door of the house open.

Henry!

A stab of guilt pierced her heart at the thought of poor, loyal Henry, whom she had left in her bed-chamber in Pemberton. Mind you, she had left him sleeping snugly upon her bed, and she knew that the spoiled little Cavalier would have detested the long journey from St Jarvis. Despite knowing that he would be most unappreciative of the plain cottage, Hestia rather wished that the little dog was there with her, as she grappled around in the dark for a tinder box and a candle. The shadows of the house felt unfamiliar, as though objects had been moved about since she had last lived there. She finally found a tinder box and the small stub of a candle, in the dresser by the kitchen window. The sense of relief she felt as the small flame threw much needed light into the darkness, was almost palpable.

She began to explore the small room, which acted as both a kitchen and sitting room, hoping to find some sticks, so that she could light a fire to throw off the cold night's air, that seemed to have permeated her very bones. She found a few, miserable twigs and set them aflame in the grate, hoping that the breeze which blew down the chimney, wouldn't extinguish them before the flames took hold.

She settled down in her mother's old chair, hoping to rest her bones, but her mind, which was usually quite practical, began to take fanciful notions, as noises from outside sent her heart racing. Ghosts are not real, she told herself, as the trees in the garden rustled in the wind. There was nothing to be afraid of, this was her home. Nothing could hurt her here; in fact nothing could hurt her as much as Alex's awful betrayal, which stung like a lash across her soul.

A particularly loud bang from the back garden caused Hestia to jump, her palms sweaty with fear. Whatever had made that noise, it was most certainly not the wind.

A fox, she thought, taking the fire poker in hand and peering out the window, or perhaps a badger. Instead of an animal, however, what she saw outside in the garden by the rockery, was a blonde haired man, who was swaying on his feet in the moonlight.

Her Uncle, Viscount Havisham.

Hestia clutched her shawl around herself and stepped out the back door into the cool night.

"Uncle," she called, her whispered voice echoing through the darkness. "Whatever are you doing?"

Havisham turned at the sound of his niece's voice, the muscles of his face slack from inebriation.

"Georgina," he slurred, as he caught sight of Hestia walking across the grass. "You're alive."

Hestia remembered, too late, the titbit of gossip that Jane had shared from London; that the Viscount Havisham had taken to the whiskey with gusto. He seemed more than drunk to her; his pale blue eyes were almost unseeing, and his mind seemed not quite right.

"I am Hestia, Uncle," she whispered uncertainly, coming to a halt a few yards away from where the drunkard stood swaying. "Georgina is gone. You came to visit just after she had died. Surely you remember?"

"She did not die," her Uncle whispered hoarsely, his face gaunt and pale. "She was murdered by that blackguard Stockbow."

"It was a low fever, which took her, Uncle," Hestia replied, taking a step back from the Viscount, whose dead eyes were beginning to unnerve her. "She was not murdered."

"She was," Havisham growled, his brow creasing in anger. "That pirate stole her from her home and murdered her. He took her from us and consigned her to a life of poverty, but I had my revenge on him."

I know what you stole Stockbow…

The words of the letter that her father had received, danced before her eyes, and a chill gripped her as she realised what his words meant.

"It was you," Hestia stated, her mind whirring with the shock of it all, "You killed my father."

The Viscount gave a bitter laugh and threw the empty bottle he held in his hand onto the grass.

"A bullet in the brain was no more than that swine deserved, for the suffering he inflicted upon my sister." Havisham growled, advancing slowly toward her. "And yet, the man has driven me demented, ever since that night. I see him in my sleep. His face, before I pulled the trigger…I see him everywhere."

Her Uncle had gone mad from guilt, Hestia realised. The Viscount ran an agitated hand through his thinning blonde hair, glancing contemptuously at his niece.

"He deserved to die; Georgina would have lived a full and prosperous life, had he not taken her away. He left her with nothing," Havisham spat.

"That's not true," tears were in Hestia's eyes, as she protested against his cruel barbs. "Nobody deserves to die that way. You will hang for what you did Uncle."

Her words seemed to cause something inside the Viscount to snap, for he lunged at her, knocking her backward into the rockery. His large hands closed around her neck and he began to squeeze, his eyes wild with anger.

"I will not hang for Stockbow," he roared, spittle at the corner of his mouth. He was no longer human, but like a daemon or a rabid animal, as his fingers clung to her neck in a vice-like grip.

Panic seized Hestia, as her Uncle's grip on her windpipe prevented any air from entering her lungs. With the last of her strength she grappled for something, anything, to fight him off with. Her hand touched a stone from the rockery and with an enormous effort, she lifted it and brought it crashing against the Viscount's long, thin, aristocratic nose, praying that it would be enough to save her.

16 CHAPTER SIXTEEN

Fury and fear drove Alex, as he urged his mount into one last gallop. He had spent the best part of the ride to Truro debating whether he would wring Hestia's neck for absconding, or simply carry her away to the nearest inn so he could rain kisses over every last inch of her body.

"Would you like to stay in my bed tonight?"

Oh, how that simple question, asked in such a sweetly innocent way, had torn at his soul. He remembered the look of hurt on his wife's face, as he had refused her offer through gritted teeth. He could not have taken her, even though he had desperately wanted to, not when he was keeping the truth from her. She had not been the only one to suffer, for he had spent the best part of the night tossing and turning, longing to sate his body's need for her.

If only she had given him a chance to explain, he though with irritation, as left Truro and took the road to Rose Cottage, instead of running away. He had returned from the library, to find her bed-chamber empty, a miserable looking Henry alone on the bed. A search of the house had yielded no sign of her, until a slight scullery maid with a lisp, had said that she had seen the Marchioness, running down the driveway.

Alex had assumed that his wife had decided to walk to St Jarvis, being fond as she was of both walking and completely ignoring his instructions. When she was not to be found at the boarding house, or at Jarvis Hall, worry had begun to set in.

The noise that he had thought he had heard at the library door—it had to have been Hestia. What had she overheard? Her husband confessing that he knew who had killed her father, yet was reluctant to share it with her?

Alex had cursed so violently, that he had been forced to apologise to the butler at Jarvis Hall.

"Is everything alright, my Lord?" the elderly man had enquired, perplexed by the sudden change in the Marquess's demeanour.

"Please tell Lord Payne that I must go, at once to Truro," he had called over his shoulder, as he chased after the groom who had just relieved him of his horse. "And send word to Pemberton that I and my wife shall not return until the morrow."

That had been early afternoon, now it was late evening and the inky black sky above his head, was part obscured by heavy, threatening, rain clouds.

"I hope she has managed to light a fire," Alex grumbled, as he guided the horse —whose name he did not know, for he was borrowed from Everleigh's stables— down the quaint country lane which led to Rose Cottage. Hestia's childhood home was the only place that he could think of that his wife might run away to. As well as hoping that she'd managed to heat the place, Alex was also hoping that she was actually there...

"Stop it!"

A wild shriek tore through the silence of the peaceful night, sending waves of panic through Alex's body. The voice was as familiar as his own; it was Hestia, and by the sound of it she was in trouble. He urged his horse on in a wild gallop, leaning low against the creature's neck, as they tore down the lane.

Once they reached the walls of Rose Cottage's garden, Alex leapt from the saddle, and crashed through the gate.

"No. Stop. Stop it."

Alex ran in the direction of Hestia's distressed voice, rounding the side of the cottage, to find his wife lying on the ground, beating at a man above her, with what looked like a stone. The blonde haired man had his hands wrapped around his wife's throat, though his efforts at choking her were being hampered by her admirable struggle and the tide of blood that washed down his nose.

"Unhand her at once, you cur," Alex roared, crossing the short distance in three long strides and grabbing the man by his collar. He hauled the scoundrel off Hestia, threw him against the wall of Rose Cottage and proceeded to rain punch after punch down upon his face.

"Alex, stop. You'll kill him if you keep hitting him like that."

A small white hand grabbed his bicep and tugged, willing him back from his furious frenzy. Alex let go of the man, who slumped unconscious to the ground, and turned to look at Hestia. His breath was ragged in his chest, and a stinging heat pricked his eyes; if he wasn't a war veteran, and a Marquess to boot, he would have sworn he was almost crying.

"Are you alright?" he asked, reaching out for his wife, whose eyes were huge and round in her deathly pale face.

"I'm fine," she whispered, tucking a strand of hair behind her ear. In her hand she still held the weapon that she had used to beat her attacker off with, clutched in such a tight grip that her knuckles were white.

"Is that Havisham?" Alex questioned, glancing down at the sorry heap of a man, slumped on the grass. The Viscount was out cold —though, from the smell of him, Alex couldn't be too certain if it was from the strength of his punches, or the strength of the alcohol the man had bathed in.

"He confessed," tears began to slide slowly down Hestia's cheeks, revulsion clear on her face as she glanced at her Uncle. "He was the one who killed my father, not Dubois. You were right."

"I don't care if I was right," Alex grunted, his heart aching for the slip of a girl before him. "All I care is that you are safe. You are my everything, Hestia. I could not bear if anything were to happen to you. I love you Hestia, with all my heart."

"I thought I was going to die," Hestia confessed, allowing him to take her free hand in his, "And then I thought how cruel a trick it would be, for me to die before I could tell you that I feel the same."

"You..?" Alex trailed off, not daring to hope.

"I love you," Hestia cried, flinging her arms around his neck. "I love you, for all your strength, kindness and compassion. I love you, even though you refused to share my bed."

"Hold on, one second," Alex gave a low growl, as he pulled her toward him. "I did not refuse, I simply could not share your bed whilst I was keeping secrets from you. How could I take all of you, when I was keeping a part of me from you?"

This seemed to mollify his wife, who gave a small mewl of approval at his words. Her blue eyes danced with happiness, and she tightened her grip around his neck.

"Oofh," Alex groaned, as the stone which she still held in her hand, thwacked the side of his ear. "You may drop your weapon, my Lady. I swear I'm not about to ravage you...just yet."

Hestia laughed and drew back, she made to drop the stone in her hand onto the grass, but before she could, Alex gave a gasp and reached out to grab her wrist.

"Wait," he whispered, taking the stone from her, his heart pounding with excitement. "Hestia, do you know what this is?"

He held the stone up for her to examine. Unlike the other stones in the garden, which were slate grey, this one was a pale yellow. It was flat and oblong shaped, and upon either side were strange etchings.

"It's not?" Hestia met his eyes, her own filled with wonder as she gazed upon the missing piece of Egyptian steele, that Alex had been searching for. "It is!"

His cries of jubilation were interrupted by the Viscount, who had begun to stir from his slumber. Alex had near forgotten about the fiend in his delight at having been reunited with Hestia, and now the resurfacing of a long-thought-lost artifact.

"I'll tie him up, and then we can ride into Truro to find the local magistrate, and have him deal with him."

In a matter of minutes, Alex had bound the Viscount's hands and feet together with yarn from inside the cottage, he then took Hestia, seated side-saddle in his lap, into town. He left his wife in the safety of a warm bedroom in the local inn, and went to wake the magistrate —who was none too happy at being woken—and took him to Havisham. When Alex finally crept back into the room that he had left his wife in, he found Hestia sleeping soundly underneath fresh white sheets. Not wishing to disturb her, he removed his boots quietly, took off his coat and shirt, and slipped into the bed beside her.

Another man might have woken her and demanded his marital rights, but for Alex, just sharing a bed with his wife and having the pleasure of watching her slumber, was enough for now.

EPILOGUE

"Verdict of Murder Returned in Death of Notorious Pirate."
The headline about her father, unlike the previous one, was much smaller and tucked away at the back of the paper. Its insignificant position probably had something to do with Viscount Havisham's family, who had managed to have the Viscount quietly declared insane, and locked away in an asylum. Havisham's young son, Alex told her, had paid the papers a pretty penny to keep his father's misdeeds unreported.
It had struck Hestia as deeply unfair; though one afternoon, when riding in Hyde Park with Alex, she had caught sight of her cousin, seen the drawn look upon his face, and decided that perhaps enough suffering had been felt by all. There was no need to pour salt onto what was clearly, for her cousin, a painful, festering wound.
Her father's remains had been removed from the pauper's grave outside Truro and re-interred in the small graveyard, beside the church near Rose Cottage.
The headstone simply read; "Here Lies David Stockbow and his beloved wife Georgina". It was apt, Hestia thought, for she knew that death had not ended her parents' love for each other. Life might end, but love does not, she had thought as she had stolen a glance at Alex, who stood by her side.
Her husband was, to her at least, a complete revelation. Gone forever was the forbidding Marquess, who had petrified her in Montagu House, replaced by a man of such honest integrity, that she often could not believe he was hers.
And he was hers; for after they had returned from St Jarvis, and finally taken their honeymoon in Penzance, Alex had set about making her legally his wife, in every way possible.
"You are blushing, wife dear," her husband said, as he strode into the dining room, fresh from washing after his morning's ride. Alex, Hestia had soon discovered, could not walk anywhere like a normal person, he strode —for he was always busy, bustling and full of energy.
"I am not blushing, husband dearest," she replied mildly, taking a sip of her tea and placing the paper upon the table, "I believe your eyes are finally giving out. It is only to be expected for a man of such advanced years as yourself…"
She gave a shriek of glee, as her husband lifted her from her seat, by her

waist.

"If my eyes are giving out, then you shall have to sit close enough for me to see you," he whispered wolfishly, sitting down and pulling her with him, so that she was perched in his lap.

"Whatever will the servants say?" Hestia mused aloud, before her husband brought his lips crashing down on hers.

"I'm sure they're already gossiping about all the time we spend in our bed-chamber," Alex snorted, as their kiss ended, "They may add kissing in the dining room, to their whispers for all I care, for I shall kiss you as I feel, m'dear."

His proclamation caused a huge smile to spread over Hestia's face; she was still delightfully enchanted by the idea that this man loved her enough that he would risk earning a reputation as the most unfashionable sort of thing: a husband in love.

"Tell me," she asked, twining her fingers into his hair. "How goes your work with Pierre?"

Pierre Dubois had been so overjoyed at the return of the missing stone, that he had easily confessed to Alex why he had not told him about his trip to Truro. It seemed that Mr Dubois *had* attempted to hire thugs to help him scare Hestia's father into revealing the stone's whereabouts, but the thugs had thought him a rather easy mark. They had taken the money he had offered, then proceeded to steal the rest of his valuables, leaving him in a ditch without a penny to his name.

It had all been rather humiliating for the proud Frenchman, though he had declared to Hestia that humiliation was what he had deserved, for attempting to hire them in the first place.

"It's all going rather well, actually," Alex confided, his handsome face smiling happily. "One side of the steele actually contained text written in Latin, which has revealed to us a sort of code. Latin words that appear more than once, correspond with symbols that appear the same amount of times. It's all terribly exciting."

"Terribly," Hestia agreed, stifling a grin. That her husband was so dedicated to his work, was charming —though not so charming that she could pretend for long that she found it interesting.

"Tell me," she continued, "When do you expect to be finished?"

"All going well," Alex replied, "We hope to be finished in half a year's time."

"That gives us plenty of time then," Hestia said, with a mysterious grin.

"Plenty of time for what?"

For a man who loved to solve puzzles, he looked terribly confused. Hestia took her husband's hand and placed it on her stomach, which was still flat as ever.

"Plenty of time to prepare, for whoever is growing in here," she whispered, looking at him a little uncertainly. Would he be as happy as she was, at the news? She did not know if she could bear him being indifferent to the tiny life that was growing within.

"You mean?"

Alex's face lit up, before a frown of worry creased his brow.

"You'll have to rest up," he said pompously, assuming the high-handed air of a Marquess. "No more walks with Henry. No more gallivanting through the park. No more…"

"Afternoons in bed together?" Hestia asked innocently, her eyebrows raised.

Realising he had been checkmated, Alex gave her a rueful smile.

"Was I being bossy?" he asked, his eyes apologetic.

"Only a little," Hestia laughed, "Though I was being stubborn. You're right, I will have to rest easy for a few months."

"Say that again," her husband deadpanned.

"Say what?"

"That I am right. It is the most wonderful thing I have ever heard you say —after I love you, of course."

Alex grabbed her hands, which were making to poke him indignantly in the chest, and covered them with his own.

"Don't say it again," he decided aloud, "Say the other thing, if you will?"

"I love you," Hestia whispered, her heart bursting with pure joy. Love, the thing that she had always feared would break her, had made her whole instead.

OTHER WORKS BY CLAUDIA STONE

Regency Black Hearts Series:

Proposing to a Duke
The Duke's Brother
A Lady Like No Other

Reluctant Regency Brides Series:

The Duke of Ruin
The Lord of Heartbreak
The Marquess of Temptation

…Not yet Released:

The Duke of Shadows
The Captain of Betrayal

If you would like to hear about Claudia's next release, simply follow her on Facebook or Instagram!

Or you can email her:

claudiastoneauthor@mail.com

Printed in Great Britain
by Amazon.